GOD'S MOUNTAIN

GOD'S
MOUNTAIN

ERRI DE LUCA

Translated from the Italian by Michael Moore

Riverhead Books
New York

Riverhead Books
Published by The Berkley Publishing Group
A division of Penguin Putnam Inc.
375 Hudson Street
New York, New York 10014

Copyright © 2001 by Giangiacomo Feltrinelli Editore Milano
Translation copyright © 2002 by Michael Moore
Book design by Tiffany Kukec

First published as *Montedidio* by Feltrinelli in Milan, Italy, in September 2001
First Riverhead trade paperback edition: December 2002

Visit our website at www.penguinputnam.com

Library of Congress Cataloging-in-Publication Data

De Luca, Erri, 1950–
    [Montedidio. English]
    God's mountain / Erri De Luca ; translated from the Italian by Michael Moore.
        p.   cm.
    ISBN 1-57322-960-1
    I. Moore, Michael, 1954 Aug. 24–   II. Title.

    PQ4864.E5498 M6613   2002
    853'.914—dc21

                                                    2002031769

Printed in the United States of America

10   9   8   7   6   5   4   3   2   1

GOD'S MOUNTAIN

'A JURNATA È 'NU MUORZO —the day is a morsel, reads the sign over the doorway to Master Errico's workshop. I'd already been standing out front for a quarter of an hour to start my first day of work off right. He gets there at seven, rolls up the gates, and speaks his words of encouragement: the day is a morsel. One bite and it's gone, so let's get busy. Yes, sir, I answer, and so it went. I'm writing my first entry today to keep track of these new days. I don't go to school anymore. I turned thirteen and my dad sent me to work. It's the right thing to do. It's time. You only have to stay in school till third grade. He let me stay until fifth because I was sickly and also because that way I'd have a better diploma. Around here all the kids go to work even if they never went to school, and Papa didn't want that. He works at the docks. He never went to school and is just learning to read and write at the night school run by the longshoremen's cooperative. He only speaks dialect and is intimidated by proper Italian and people with an education. He says that you do better in life if you know Italian. I know Italian because I read library books, but I don't speak it. I write in Italian because it's quiet. I can put down what happens every day, sheltered from the noise of Neapolitan.

I'M FINALLY working, even if I don't make much, and Saturdays I bring home my pay. It's the beginning of summer. At six in the morning it's cool. The two of us have breakfast together and then I put on my smock. We leave the house together. I walk up the street with him a ways and then head back. Master Errico's shop is in the alley down from our building. For my birthday Papa gave me a piece of curved wood. It's called a boomerang. I took it in my hands without asking what it was. A tingle, a little electric shock went through me. Papa explained that you throw it far and it always comes back. Mama was against it. *"Ma addò l'adda ausa";* where's he gonna use it? She's right. In this neighborhood of alleyways called Montedidio there's not enough room to spit between your feet, no room to hang out the wash. All right, I said, maybe I can't throw it, but I can still practice the moves. It's heavy, like iron. Mama gave me a pair of long trousers. She got them at the market in Resina. They're good quality. American. Rugged, dark. I put them on and rolled them up to my knees. "Now you're a man," an *ommo,* "you bring money home." Yes, I bring home my pay on Saturdays, but it'll take a lot more than that to make me a man. Meantime I've lost my voice and have a frog in my throat.

~ ~ ~

PAPA GOT the boomerang from a sailor friend. It's not a *pazziella*, a toy. It's a tool that ancient people used. As he explains, I get to know its surface. I rub my hand over it, in the direction of the grain. From Master Errico I learn about the grains of wood. There's a right way and a wrong way. I follow the boomerang's grain when I polish it and it shakes a little in my hands. It's not a toy, but it's not a tool either. It's something in between, a weapon. I want to learn how to use it. I want to practice throwing it tonight, after Mama and Papa have gone to sleep. Italian has one word for sleep and another for dream. Neapolitan has just one—*suonno*. For us they're the same thing.

~ ~ ~

I SWEPT the floor of the woodshed today and got attacked by fleas. They went for my legs. At work I wear shorts, and my legs turned black. Master Errico stripped me and washed me down at the pump in front of the shop. We were laughing like crazy. Thank goodness it's summer. There were mice in the woodshed, too. We put down some poison. " 'O súrece! 'O súrece!" he screamed. They give him the creeps, not me. Then I got paid. He counted out the money and gave it to me. At night I started to practice with the boomerang. I learned that it didn't come from America. It came from Australia. The Americans are full of new things. The Neapolitans gather around when their ships weigh anchor and they come ashore. The latest thing is a plastic circle. It's called the Hula Hoop. I saw Maria spinning it around on her hips without letting it fall to the ground. She told me, "Try it." I said no, that I didn't think it was for boys. Maria turned thirteen before me.

She lives on the top floor. That was the first time she talked to me.

I SQUEEZE the boomerang. It gives me a shock. I start going through the moves to throw it. I wind it around behind my shoulder, then thrust it forward like I'm going to release it, but I don't. My shoulders are quick, like Maria's hips. I can't let the boomerang fly free. We're too cramped on top of Montedidio. My hand grips the last half inch of the wood and pulls it behind me. I keep doing this, back and forth. My back loosens up. I work up a sweat. I keep a tight grip. All it takes is a flick of the wrist for it to slip from your fingers. After a while I can see that my right hand's getting bigger than my left, so I change hands. This way one side of my body keeps up with the other, equal in speed, strength, and exhaustion. My last few unreleased throws really want to fly. It hurts my wrist to hold them back, so I stop.

I DIDN'T want to stay at school. I was bigger than the other fifth graders. At snack time some kids used to take cakes out of their bags. To us poor kids, the janitor would hand out bread with quince jam. When it got hot the poor kids would come to school with their heads shaved like melons, on account of lice. The other kids still had hair to comb. There were too many differences between us. They went on in school. We didn't. I had to repeat grades a lot because I used to get sick with fevers. Then they promoted me but I didn't want to go to school anymore. I wanted to help out, to work. The studying I've done is enough. I know Italian, a quiet language that sits still inside books.

~ ~ ~

EVER SINCE I started working and training with the boomerang I get hungrier. Papa is happy to have breakfast with me. At six the first rays of sunlight slither into the street and make their way into the houses, even the lower floors. We don't turn the light on. In summer the sunlight treads lightly over the ground before climbing up and becoming an oven that sits on top of the city. I put bread inside my cup of milk, which is darkened with coffee substitute. Papa used to get up alone every morning and now he's happy that I'm there, to talk to, to leave the house with. Mama gets up late. A lot of the time she's weak. At lunchtime I go up to the washbasins on the roof to hang out the laundry, then I pick it up in the evening. I never used to go up to the terrace before. It's high above Montedidio and gets a little breeze in the evening. No one can see me so I practice there. The boomerang quivers in the fresh air. My sleeve gets twisted when I squeeze the boomerang to keep from letting go. It's wood that was grown to fly. Master Errico is a good carpenter. He says that wood is good for fire, for water, for wine. I know that it's good for flying, too, but I won't say so if he won't. I was thinking I'd like to throw the boomerang from where the washbasins are, from the highest rooftop in Montedidio.

MY ARMS are tired, sweaty, so I stretch out for a bit on the pavement by the clotheslines. By now there isn't even a sliver of the city above me. I close my good eye, and look up with the other one, the blind one, half open. Instantly the sky grows darker, denser, closer, right on top of me. My right eye is weak, but it can see the sky better than my good eye, which I need for the street, to look people in the face, to do my job in the shop. My left eye is sly, fast, understands things in a heartbeat. It's Neapolitan. My right is slow. It can't focus on anything. Instead of clouds it sees the scattered tufts of the mattress maker in the street, when he combs and twists the wool and breaks it up into tufts on a sheet spread out on the ground.

I GO back to the washbasins, carrying the clothes basket. In the darkness of the stairs someone spies me going by. I can feel other people's eyes, even in the dark, because when they touch, when they look, it's like a slight current of air passing under a door. I think it's Maria. The building is old. Spirits pass you on the stairs. Once their bodies are gone, spirits start to miss their hands. The desire to touch makes them throw themselves at people. Despite all the effort they put into it, all you feel is a caress. Now that it's summer they rub against my face. They dry away the sweat. Spirits are happy in old buildings. But if someone says they saw them they're lying. You can only feel spirits, and only when they want.

MASTER ERRICO gives space in his shop to a cobbler named Don Rafaniello. I clean up his space, too, around the workbench and the pile of shoes that he fixes. He came to Naples from somewhere in Europe after the war. He went straight to Montedidio to Master Errico's and started fixing the shoes of the poor. He makes them new again. They call him Rafaniello because his hair is red, his eyes are green, he's short, and he has a hump on the top of his back. In Naples, it took one look for them to nickname him *ravanello*, radish. That's how he became Don Rafaniello. Not even he knows how many years he's been in the world.

KIDS DON'T understand age. For them forty and eighty are all the same mess. Once on the stairs I heard Maria ask her grandma if she was old. He grandma said no. Maria asked if her grandpa was old. Her grandma answered no. Then Maria asked, "So there's no such thing as old people," and got smacked across the face. I can tell how old people are, except for Rafaniello. His face is a hundred, his hands are forty, his hair, all red and bushy, twenty. From his words, I can't tell. He doesn't talk much, and when he does, it's in a teeny tiny voice. He sings in a foreign language. When I sweep up his corner he smiles at me, making his wrinkles and freckles ripple like the sea in the rain.

~ ~ ~

HE'S A good man, Rafaniello. He fixes the shoes of the poor and won't take money from them. One guy came by who wanted a new pair. Rafaniello took his measurements with a piece of string, made a few knots, and got to work. The guy came back to try them on for size and there they were. They fit like a glove. Rafaniello cares about people's feet. He wouldn't hurt a fly, so the flies never bother him. They buzz around him but never land on his skin, no matter how many there are. Master Errico shakes his neck like a carriage horse to get them out of his face when his hands are busy. He even snorts like a horse. I swat a rag around him and they leave him alone for a second.

~ ~ ~

I WEAR sandals even in winter. My feet are growing and this way they can stick out a little without having to buy a new pair. They're small on me. I sweep the floor in my bare feet, so as not to wear them out. Rafaniello took them one morning, and when I put them on at noon they fit me so well I was afraid they were the wrong sandals. I looked at him and he nodded yes, yes, with his head. I tell him, thank you Don Rafaniè. He answers, "You don't have to call me don." But you're a good Christian. You do acts of charity for the feet of the poor. You deserve to be called don. "No, call other people don if you want to. I'm not even a Christian. Where I'm from I had a name that was almost the same as Rafaniello." I didn't say a word. Till then we'd almost never spoken. The sandal leather smelled nice. It had come back to life in his hands. At home Mama complimented me, saying that I was good at getting people to like me. But with Don Rafaniello it doesn't count. He likes everybody.

~ ~ ~

I HEAR screeches and Neapolitan voices. I speak Neapolitan but I write Italian. "We're in Italy," Papa says, "but we're not Italian. To speak the language we have to study it, like being abroad, in America, but without leaving home. Many of us will never speak Italian and will die in Neapolitan." It's a hard language, he says, but you will learn it and be Italian. Me and your mother won't. *"Noi nun pu, nun po, nuie nun putimmo."* He's trying to say "we can't," *non possiamo,* but the words won't come out. I tell him how to say it the Italian way. "Good boy," he says, "good boy. You know the national language." Sure I know it and I even write it in secret and when I do, I feel a little like I'm cheating on Neapolitan, so in my head I conjugate the verb "can," *potere. I' pozzo, tu puozzi, isso po', nuie putimmo, vuie putite, lloro ponno.* Mama doesn't agree with Papa and says, "We're Neapolitans and that's all there is to it." *"Ll'Italia mia,"* she says, doubling the *l* of the article.

"*Ll'Italia mia sta in America*"—my Italy is in America. That's where half my family lives. "Your homeland is what puts food on your plate," she says, and stops. To tease her, Papa says, "Then you must be my homeland." He doesn't want to disagree with Mama. In our house we never raise our voices, we don't get into arguments. If something bothers him, he puts his hand over his mouth and covers half his face.

MASTER ERRICO has me spreading pore-filler on wood and sanding it down. Then I polish the doors of a wardrobe for clothes. How many clothes does this family have? We're making eight doors, two levels. They call it a "four seasons." Today I tested the latch on the first door and it fit so well that it made a vacuum sound. The air escaped from inside. Master Errico made me put my face near the door. I could feel the air stroking my cheek. That's how the spirits rub up against my face.

Then Master Errico took it apart and covered it. It's a big job. He's been tinkering with it for a year. The drawers are made out of beech, the joints are dovetailed. It feels great to run your hands over them. He checks the squaring again and again, greasing the runners until the drawers don't make a sound when he pulls them out and slides them back in. He says it's like dropping a fishing line in the sea. They rise and fall silently in his hands. Master Errico, I say, you're a genius, a fishing cabinet maker.

EVERY DAY Master Errico buys the paper *Il Mattino*. It's an expense, thirty lira, but a man's got to know what's happening in the world, he says. He reads some of the news out loud to us: the sword fell out of the hands of the statue of Roger the Norman that guards the Royal Palace. In Genoa there was a big riot between the police and the factory workers. Master Errico's voice is strong. The pieces he reads stay with me. On Sundays he goes fishing, dropping a line from a rowboat off the port. All day long he sits quietly in the traffic of the ships going by. He waits until a *sarago* surrenders. *Sarago* swim near the breakwater, believe it or not, beneath the black sheet of water. They're down there, he says, as crafty as street urchins. There's an art to robbing them from the sea. For bait you use mussels. One day he'll teach me. "I'll learn you," he says.

SARAGO NEVER sits on our table. We eat anchovies. *Sarago* is expensive, but Master Errico brings it home every Sunday and cooks it in crazy water. "Heaven and the sea allowing," he says. He manages by himself. He's sixty and doesn't wear glasses. He strains his eyes, and has to measure what he's going to cut again and again, be careful. The boy he used to have was good, but he

18

hung out with the Mob when he was growing up and now he's doing time. That's how I ended up here. I lend him my eyes. I mark down the inches. Then he calculates how much he needs to cut and corrects the measurement.

I SPEND my days cleaning the tools, the machines, getting rid of wood chips, sawdust. Exercising with the boomerang is making me stronger. My shoulders are filling out my shirt, a ripple of muscles presses against the cloth of the back, and there's a long callus along my palms where I squeeze the wooden handle. In the evening up by the washbasins I throw harder and harder. I go through the whole motion of throwing it and then at the last minute I squeeze, at the end of the run from my shoulders to my arm. My thrust gets stronger. The boomerang is itching to fly away. My palms sweat, giving off a smell of bitter wood, more bitter than chestnut. No one sees me, only the spirits that blow an occasional dry kiss to my face. The street is noisy even at night, but I'm higher than anyone, up among the clotheslines, where the loudest noise is the boomerang's edge slicing the air as it passes my ears.

RAFANIELLO IS tired. He sleeps badly and his hump is burning. But he's happy. He says it's a good sign. He confides in me when Master Errico goes out to buy wood. He tells me his story. He came to Naples by mistake. He had wanted to go to Jerusalem after the war. He got off the train and saw the sea for the first time. A ship blew its whistle and he remembered a festival in his hometown that began with the same sound. He looked at people's feet, at how many bare feet there were, lots of children like in his town, so skinny, fast, they could be his own. He comes from a hard-luck town that lost all its children. The crowds in Naples remind him of them. There are so few people in his old town they don't even say hello to one another anymore. In Naples you could spend all day saying hello to people and go to bed tired just from that.

RAFANIELLO TOOK a walk around our city—foreign, yet almost like his own used to be before the war. The same faces, shouts, insults, and curses, and he thought it was strange that he couldn't understand a word. He touched his ears to see if something was wrong with them. He laughs when he tells me about it. He gave up. The city was foreign. He thought the sea was holding the city back, refusing to let it leave. So he, too, had to stay. He couldn't walk the rest of the way to Jerusalem, and the ships here set sail for America, not the Holy Land. So he stays, telling himself: I'll stay for a while. It's late 1945. There's a need for shoes. People want to get married. Naples is filled with weddings. So Rafaniello stays and waits. The stories he tells in the workshop cast a spell on me. I have to pinch myself to get back to work.

EACH OF us has an angel. That's what Rafaniello says. And angels don't travel. If you go away, you lose your angel and have to find another one. In Naples he ends up with a slow angel. It doesn't fly, it walks. Right away it tells him, "You can't go to Jerusalem." What do I have to wait for? Rafaniello asks. "Dear Rav Daniel," the angel answers him, using Rafaniello's original name, "you will fly to Jerusalem on wings. I'm going to walk there, even though I'm an angel. But you will fly all the way to the Western Wall of the city on a pair of wings that are as strong as a vulture's." And who's going to give them to me? Rafaniello demands. "You already have them," the angel says. "They're in a case inside your hump." Rafaniello is sad not to be leaving, but happy about the hump he's been carrying on his back like a sack of potatoes and bones that he could never put down. They're wings, wings, he tells me, making his voice even softer. His freckles crinkle around his green eyes, which are staring up at the skylight.

THE ANGEL repeated itself, because humans have to be told everything twice. "You'll fly there on your own wings and be making shoes alongside Rav Iohanàn hassàndler," whom we call Don Giuvanni the shoemaker. What was your hometown angel like? I asked him. It knew how to make vodka from snow, he answered. I know what snow is. There was a snowfall in '56 that cleaned up the city. Naples was never whiter. "Snow doesn't clean, it covers, making everything the same.

It doesn't sweep anything away," Rafaniello instructs me, and I hold my tongue.

I LISTEN to his stories. I want to tell him that I can fly, too, but only over Naples. I want to tell him how you do it, how you position your body, that it's all in the eyes; when you look up your body goes up, when you look down, it goes down. I want to tell him what I learned in a dream, but I stay quiet. I only know how to float on the air. He does the serious stuff with the wings. Then Master Errico comes back. I throw out the rough boards but the splinters don't hurt me anymore. My skin's gotten as tough as leather. Rafaniello's stories pump my bones full of air and make me cheerful, as cheerful as a flier. In the evening by the washbasins my arms want to fly away with the boomerang. I check my thrust and holding it back makes my new muscles stronger, shaping them like a slingshot.

~ ~ ~

MASTER ERRICO says that fishermen don't know how to swim. Swimming's for vacationers who jump in the waves for fun and lie in rows under the sun. The sun is only good for people who lie there without moving. For someone who carries the sun around on his back from early morning to night, the sun is a sack of coal. Like Rafaniello's hump, I think. I think but I don't say. I'm just a shop boy. I can't go around saying what I think to my boss. And if I keep my mouth shut he keeps telling stories and the day goes by faster. Fishermen go to sea in a motorboat or a rowboat and don't even get their faces wet. They wear berets on their heads that don't come off in the wind. The old men at the docks smell like tobacco and sweat, not salt. On Sundays they all come out in white shirts. There's not much fish in the bay. To catch some they have to stay in a boat all day. I'd like to learn more about the sea. I don't know it. I see it but I don't know it. Master Errico likes talking to me. His last assistant got sick of listening to him. He'd keep on talking, but "a day is a morsel," he sighs. To end the conversation he says that sea salt is as bitter as sweat, and neither is any good for pasta.

FROM THE darkness by the washbasins Maria emerges. Her thirteen years are more mature than mine. She's already got a grown-up body. Three inches below the bangs of her short black hair is her mouth, which is fast with words. I can almost see the words spouting from her fat lips. Her smile opens up her face from ear to ear. Maria knows how to move like a woman. I stand in front of her and my stomach feels empty. I'm hungry for bread, to take a bite out of her slice of bread and butter. She offers me some. I say no. She's discovered that I practice with the boomerang. She's curious. She hears me climbing the stairs, passing by her door. She comes closer. The evening is warm and scented with chocolate, oregano, and cinnamon. I sniff at the air. It's French perfume, she says, rolling the *r*s in her throat.

IT's DARK. I grip the wood of the boomerang and show it to her. Maria knows what it is, knows what it can do. "But you don't let it fly. Why don't you throw it?" I'd lose it. "It's no good if it doesn't fly." I don't know how to answer her. I come up here to get myself ready for a single throw. One night my arm will be strong and I won't be able to stop and then the boomerang will fly. I think for a while and say, You keep canaries on your balcony and don't let them fly. I keep my boomerang locked up, too. "But they sing," Maria says. The boomerang whistles, I say, and make her place her ear close so she can hear the sound of the wind being sliced by my throw. Don't be scared. She laughs. She opens the hand that I have tight around the boomerang and touches my fingers. I gulp. The boomerang's in her hands now. Wow, I can't believe how heavy it is, she says, and gives it back to me. Heavy? It's a wooden wing, how can it be heavy? She insists that it's heavy and that it burns, too. She knows why I'm practicing, she touches my shoulders. "You've gotten strong since you started to work." I lower my eyes. Maria takes the hair hanging over my forehead and pulls it up. "Look at me when I talk to you." It's dark and Maria's getting bold with me. She's a little taller and her breasts are already sticking out. I stand still for a while, then I pry her fingers from my hair. She walks away, turns around, and says, "Come back this time tomorrow. I want to tell you a secret." I stay there by myself. The night air is refreshing near the washbasins rinsed clean with soap flakes. This is where the mothers wash the dirty clothes and their children's cuts. I take the clothes off the line and go downstairs.

~ ~ ~

MAMA SLEEPS a lot. From one day to the next she comes down with jaundice. She's as yellow as old garlic. I dip my bread in cold milk. I'm not allowed to turn on the gas. Papa's gone off to get medicine. He has to look all over Naples before he can find a pharmacy that's open at ten o'clock at night. I keep the boomerang near the kitchen table. It's always with me, or on me. At work I keep it under my jacket. New things are on the way. Rafaniello, Maria, the strength I'm getting at the wash-basins. The boomerang comes from the sea. It has to fly. In the meantime it's building the muscles of a kid who still smells like an ink pot at school. He's been working since June with a carpenter and he writes down the new happenings in his life with a pencil on a scroll of paper given to him by the Montedidio print shop, left over from a big reel of newsprint. I turn the scroll and can already see things written down from the past, things that roll up before my eyes.

~ ~ ~

MASTER ERRICO sings. When he works hard he starts up with a song and doesn't stop. He consumes it. Rafaniello sings, too, but silently, inside his throat. He doesn't move his lips much and is holding a dozen shoe tacks for soles in the corner of his mouth. I can hear him even over the voice of Master Errico, which gets louder as the day gets longer and stops at noon, lunchtime, when the room is lit by a ray of sun that splits it in two. The sawdust rises in the air to meet the visiting light.

Rafaniello sings nice, even when the buzz saw or planing machine is going. I can always tell if he's singing or not. What songs do you know, Don Rafaniè? I ask. He used to know a lot of them; now he only sings one. I was taught not to ask too many questions and to keep my curiosity to myself. He lets a little silence go by, enough for me to ask a second question, then he answers. He says that he only sings one song, and just a few verses. The words are a good-luck wish for building a kind of house where you pray. A church, I say. No, a house where you read, you study, and you say a prayer. Rafaniello smiles, he wants to end our conversation. The day is a morsel, and there are plenty of shoes to fix.

MASTER ERRICO squints because of the dust, because of the risk of getting a splinter in his eye. He's got crow's-feet from the strain of closing them. Rafaniello's eyes are moist. He dries them with the back of his hand. He's started to confide in me. Don Rafaniè, you look like you're crying. "It's the air in here," he says. "It's the glue. It's Montedidio wringing out my eyes." And he dries them. He says that all eyes need tears to see. Otherwise they get like fish eyes, which don't see anything once they're out of the water, and they dry up, blinded. Tears are what allow us to see. They come without being forced by crying. I nod yes with my head and feel two teardrops pinching at the top of my nose, trying to come out. They're tickling me to make me cry. I turn around quick, blow my nose into my hands, throw the snot down on the ground into the sawdust, sweep it up. I have to force myself because I'm ashamed and I throw in a bit of Neapolitan, which always comes in handy. *"Che chiagne a ffà?"* I tell myself. What're you crying for? I spit on the ground but the two teardrops well up anyway. Master Errico notices. *"Guagliò to scorre la parpétola."* Kid, your eyelids are leaking. He tells me to come out of the back of the workshop. He sends me out to get a half jar of axle grease at Don Liborio's print shop. On the street I can see more clearly. The fruit peels, the gills of the fish, the swordfish split in two, the tin plate of a beggar who stands up all day long and doesn't sit down because the passersby are standing, and they hate to see panhandlers getting too comfortable on the ground. Rafaniello's right. All it takes is two teardrops to clear your eyesight.

~ ~ ~

DON LIBORIO gives me the grease and tries to goose
me, to grab my *piscitiello*. I can't do anything about it.
There's not much he can do anyway. I'm strong and
can slip out of his grip in a snap. He's heavy, slow, and
tries to goose all the guys. He chuckles more like a dove
than a man. He runs the print shop by himself. None
of the guys wants to get near him. People know, but
they mind their own business, and Don Liborio is someone who does good deeds. He paid for the wedding
gown of an orphan who had no dowry. And people say
that no one ever died from getting goosed. *"Quanno è
pé vizio, nun é peccato."* No harm done when it's done
out of habit. That's how they see it. Master Errico sends
me there because he knows Don Liborio will give me
the grease. But he tells me, "Come back quickly, don't
be wasting time with him." So I come back quickly.
Don Liborio's got a habit of grabbing guys' crotches.
That's what turns him on. He gave me the scroll of
newsprint that I'm writing on. Walking along, I lose

the effect of the teardrops. Everything looks dirty. I hold the boomerang close to my chest. Who knows what Don Liborio would have felt if I had stuck it down my pants. That night, at home, it's quiet. Mama is sleeping. I eat a little bread dipped in milk. We don't cook without her. Papa chews on some bread, oil, and tomato. I say good night and climb up the stairs to practice and to take the clothes off the line.

MARIA COMES upstairs, too. We sit down under the bare clotheslines. I'm all sweaty and the boomerang is hot from all the air it's sliced. Maria touches me. She doesn't say anything. She touches me, first around my body and then over my trousers. I don't know how to make any moves. I just look. She grabs me in one place and I have trouble keeping my eyes open. I want to close them, to breathe deep, but I force myself not to give in. I keep them open so that I can at least reciprocate with my eyes, since I don't know how to do anything else. It's dark. I look at her serious face. She moves her hand around on the same spot. I don't understand what's happening down there. She doesn't look at me. I don't take my eyes off her face. I don't look to see where she's touching me. She's stroking something that's mine. It's not the same *piscitiello* that Don Liborio touched. It's in the same place, but it's some other flesh that's grown out of me to meet the strokes she's making with her smooth hands. Then Maria isn't looking at her hand anymore. She's looking at me looking at her, and slowly, slowly she starts to smile, and when I see her smile, I feel like I've been punched in the stomach, a coughing inside my flesh, a fling of the boomerang that's slipped out of my hands and emptied me.

~ ~ ~

I LOOK for it and it's lying there on the ground, nearby. Maria stops, gets out a handkerchief, dries her hand, of what I don't know, maybe of sweat, like I do after practice. My blind right eye also got wet from straining to keep it open. Then I look down and see flesh that I'd never seen before, a long dry tube, a little crooked, where my *piscitiello* used to be. If it weren't for Maria, who is all calm, I'd be screaming from the shock. But she's there and plants a kiss on my lips, under my nose. I'm nice to her, quiet. I don't ask what happened. Above us the clotheslines cut the August sky into ribbons. I'm glad that there aren't any sheets or balconies above us. We're on the highest rooftop in Montedidio.

~ ~ ~

"I DO this to the landlord," she says. Do what? It bothers me to hear the name of the landlord, the most annoying person I know. He asks the tenants, "When will you pay me," when other people can hear. "When will you pay me?" he says real loud, to embarrass them.

"What I did for you I do for him," Maria says. I hold my tongue so I won't say anything stupid. "Tonight I wanted to touch a clean body, look at a face that looks back at me, that respects me. Now you're my boyfriend and I won't let the landlord touch me anymore. I won't do anything for him, not even if he throws us out of the building." Is that what he said, that he would throw you out? "No, that's what my mother says, because we've got debts. People come around to our house to ask us to pay up." I keep quiet, even if I don't understand everything. I can see that Maria is happy to stay with me up by the washbasins. She even likes the boomerang. She acts like she's going to throw it, gets a shock, and shrieks with joy and amazement. How can I play with it when it's so heavy? It can't be heavy, I tell her, it's made for flying. "Are you going to make it fly?" Yes, I tell her. She asks when; I still don't know. "When you do, can I come, too?" I don't answer. The boomerang isn't a toy. It's a big secret. When it flies it'll break away from my arm, in a farewell to all the muscles it helped build. It'll make a lot of noise. It might hit someone; they'll look for the culprit. Who does the boomerang belong to? And they'll come up here on top of Montedidio and I'll answer that it was me, I was the one who threw the boomerang. I keep these thoughts to myself. Maria can't know them. She takes my head in her hands, places it on her breast. I feel the swelling of her flesh pushing her breath out and the tough beating of her heart. It sounds like someone knocking on the door, and I want to answer, Come in.

~ ~ ~

MARIA BREATHES deeply. My head rises and falls on her breast. She says that now it's all right, that now she's doing what makes men happy, but she's doing it for me. This way it's nice. Not like the nasty old body of the landlord, moving on top of her. Maria's body shivers, shudders, as if she's shaking out a tablecloth. She opens her eyes. I see her face turn sad. So I take the boomerang, place it so that its tips are pointing down, and pull my lips into a frown with two fingers, in a caricature of her face. Then I turn the boomerang around so that its tips are up. It turns into a smile and I smile, too. Maria comes behind us, the boomerang and me. Her mouth widens and opens her face. She embraces my head. When she loosens her arms from around me, she leaves.

~ ~ ~

RAFANIELLO RUBS his hump against the wall. It's itching him. He works quickly. He has to finish repairing the shoes of the poor. Winter begins in August, is what we say. Shoes make a big difference to your health. They come to him with worn-out, unmatched clogs. He fixes them and recommends that they wash their feet. Shoes last longer when your feet are clean. It's all right to wash them in the sea. There aren't many fountains in Naples. Rafaniello doesn't mind the smell of rotten leather, sores, or blackened feet. His nose must be sainted. But Master Errico can't stand the stench, so he's always making him move the bag of shoes from one corner to another. I help Rafaniello, but I have to hold my breath when I throw the bag over my shoulders.

He huddles over his work. His red freckles are brighter when his green eyes are calm. He tells me that at night his wing bones squeak inside his hump. They're trying to move and they hurt. It's starting.

~ ~ ~

ACCORDING TO his calculations there are two thousand kilometers of flight from Naples to Jerusalem. You think you can fly that far over the sea? He doesn't answer me. You have to build yourself up. You should eat like migratory birds do before they leave. Then I think to myself, without telling him, that if everything goes well he'll make it to Castellamare di Stabia, on the other side of the Bay. They'll mistake him for a vulture, shoot him, and stuff him with straw. What an awful thought. No, no. Rafaniello will circle the world on fresh wings, he can make it, as long as he eats something more hearty. Beat yourself a couple of eggs. With a little sugar they'd even give *me* the energy to fly. Rafaniello looks at me with his wide green eyes. "From the way the wings are moving they must be huge." We go back to work, him with nails in his mouth, me with the broom. I clean up his area, and when I'm behind him I hear a crunching of bone in his hump and think of the boomerang. It's itching to fly, too. I'll have to introduce them. He told me the secret of his hump and I still haven't confided in him.

WHERE HE lives, in a room that used to be a closet, there's no electricity. At night he lights a candle. He sets it on a chair. He says that it has to be low because light wants to rise. He also says that the candle illuminates the dark; it doesn't drive it out. From the flame, the glass of wine in the window absorbs the light, the oil shines, the bread becomes fragrant. What else do you eat? I ask. Onion, he says. When it's nice and close to the candle, you feel like kissing it rather than cutting it. Then he adds oregano. The salt sparkles when he drops a pinch from his fingertips onto the plate. While he's telling me about these ordinary things I realize that I've never seen them by candlelight before. They look even tastier, more nutritious. They'll be enough for him to fly to Jerusalem. Then he says that the room gets bigger when there's just one flame. Shadows move along the wall and keep him company. He says that in winter the candle also heats the room. Late in the evening I write down these things about Rafaniello and then I turn off the light. Mama and Papa don't like candles. They had to use them during the war.

MAMA HAS been taken to the hospital. The house doesn't make a sound, nothing moves. I can't stay there. I wash the floor and grind a little coffee for Papa just to make some noise of my own. Now I'm allowed to turn on the gas. I cook some pasta, so he'll find it ready when he comes home. I have the key to the door, too. All I had to do was make it to thirteen and right away I'm one of the men. I've lost every last bit of childishness I had. Even my voice. Now my breathing is hoarse. I rattle my voice around in my throat, but it doesn't come out sounding nice. It's buried under the ashes of my earlier voice. I try to clear my throat, but nothing. A sleepy voice comes out, like someone who just woke up and is saying their first words of the day. I'm always hoarse.

My hands are changing more than the rest of me. Now they can hold on tight, they're wide enough to grip the boomerang. The wood's losing weight. I deliver it to my arms, my fists, my fingers. I don't have a target. I don't have to hit something. I have the open air, the warm air scented with soap flakes. Some autumn night when it's cooler and the houses close their windows, I'll make the throw. I won't even see an inch of flight, but every night I get ready, a hundred times each arm.

~ ~ ~

IN THE dark Maria comes up to the washbasins. She doesn't touch me. She doesn't tempt my *piscitiello* away from my body. She told the landlord she'd had enough. He took it badly and threatened eviction. Maria's parents owe him back rent. Maria spat at his feet and left. She plucked up her courage. Just became a woman and already she knows disgust. I've had it with this game, she said, of him calling her princess, dressing her in the clothes of his dead wife, putting precious things on her, and then touching her and asking her to touch him back. Now she doesn't want it anymore because I'm here. I'm here. It makes me feel important. Till now my being around or not didn't make a bit of difference. Maria says that I'm here. Before you know it, I'll realize that I'm here, too. I wonder whether I couldn't have realized this by myself. I guess not. I guess it takes another person to tell you.

~ ~ ~

SITTING DOWN on the ground below the wall near the washbasins, Maria makes me put my hands on her breasts. It's a little crooked, uncomfortable, but I leave them there. The dark bangs over her forehead pick up a fresh breeze from the east. It dries her face. We look at each other without saying anything for long minutes. I didn't know that it was so nice just to look, to look at each other closely. I squeeze my good eye shut. With the other one I don't see as clearly, but my nose wakes up, taking in the sweaty odor of Maria and the bitterness of the wood from the boomerang in my arms. She shuts one of her eyes, too, and then switches to the other and we stare at each other and then burst out laughing at the faces we're making to change the light in our eyes. Tonight she told me, "I care for you." I care for her, too, but I don't know how to express it so well and I can't even answer. So I say nothing.

~ ~ ~

THE LANDLORD went knocking on Maria's door. She opened and he begged her, begged her, begged her on his knees to go back to him. Maria went "ntz" with her tongue and pulled her head back, spitting out the word *no*. From the kitchen her mother asked who it was, then the landlord started making a scene like he was going to send for the bailiffs from the courthouse to confiscate the furniture, and her mother begged him not to, got on her knees, too, and Maria was the only one who wasn't on her knees and who knew that the knees were wasting their time since she would never go back to the old man. I ask whether her mother knows about our visits. She doesn't answer. She opens her hands and plants a kiss under my nose. "You're my boyfriend, my family. If they evict us I'll run away and come to your house." Being boyfriend and girlfriend gives you heavy thoughts.

~ ~ ~

THERE ARE still clothes on the line. Someone might be coming to take them down. "They're mine," Maria says. "I brought them up as an excuse to get out of the house. I've started washing, ironing. That way Mama can go look for rent money." How is it that your family can't manage to pay the rent and is better off than mine? I ask. They get mixed up in gambling, the lottery, the numbers, football pools. They've got debts, she says. "But I'm not bringing the back rent to the landlord anymore. He counts it up and says it isn't enough. She can go."

MARIA DOESN'T go to church on Sundays. She says that she can't tell her confessor the things she's seen, she can't ask for Communion. I tell her that the landlord goes to church, confesses, and receives the host. "He and the priest are the same age. Between the two of them they work it out. What I need is a thirteen-year-old confessor who knows about disgust, who knows what it's like to be our age, who knows that we're puppets in the hands of grown-ups, that we don't count for anything." The Heavenly Father sees Maria, I tell her. "Yeah, He sees everything, but if I don't take care of fixing things myself, He just sits there and watches the show." I can only bite my tongue at her blasphemy. I turn red, as if I were the Heavenly Father who saw and did not help.

MY THROWING muscles get harder. Now I'm here for you, we're engaged, I say, and for that matter, Maria, what do people do when they're engaged? "They make love, get married, run away together," she says, sure of herself. I don't ask her again. It's enough for me that she knows. We look at each other. Our eyes are wide because of the dark. She cracks a smile and the tip of my *piscitiello* moves by itself. When she opens her mouth and shows me her teeth I get itchy and hot down there. I slip my arm around her shoulder, squeeze a little. It's the first time that I've touched her, that the moves have come from me. Maria rests her whole head on my arm, I can't see her face anymore, the itching of my piscitiello calms down. I feel a huge force inside. Practicing for the big throw has even given me a muscle to hold Maria. She stands up, gathers to her breast the clothes hanging on the line, and pushes her neck forward for a kiss goodbye. Then I go with my mouth aimed right at hers, so we're equal. Boyfriend and girlfriend make the same moves.

~ ~ ~

AT THE workshop I take the boomerang out from under my jacket and leave it in plain sight. Master Errico squeezes it, turns it around, sniffs at it. "It's thick," he says, then he spits on top and rubs the saliva in with his thumb. I'm shocked by his familiarity. The boomerang is ancient, it's foreign, it's a weapon. How dare he do this? He shows me the spot where he rubbed, it's turning violet, he puts his mouth over it. "It's full of tannen. It's acacia." I tell him how I got it. It's not good to work with. It's too hard. You could break a planer on it. You couldn't even carve a crutch out of it. It's not good for the stove. It must be good for something, but he doesn't know what. He gives it back to me and gets an electric shock as he lays it in my hand. He jumps in surprise: is it electric? I didn't feel anything, I lie, because I'm used to the tingling of the boomerang. Master Errico makes a dark face like he does when he doesn't understand why something went wrong. Then he comes out with his motto: *"Iamme, vuttammo 'e mmane"*; let's go, get a move on it. *" 'A iurnata è 'nu muorzo."*

I LEFT the boomerang near Rafaniello. The mountain of broken shoes starts to dwindle. In his hands they walk away by themselves. The grease makes them shine; you smell the scent of happy leather. At noon, when Master Errico goes to lunch, the poor come by to pick up their repaired shoes. With the arrival of the first cool evenings their troubles seem to get worse. They cover themselves in army blankets, two jackets, or all their shirts if they've got nothing else. "Don Rafaniè, the Heavenly Father is gonna make you rich as the sea," they say to repay him in words for what they can't pay in money, along with blessings for his health, or against gossips and the evil eye. "May you be protected from fire, earth, and evildoers," "May gold rain from your hump." Rafaniello is happy. He says that blessings are worth more than money because they are heard in heaven. Curses are heard, too, he says, and spits on the ground to rinse his mouth of the sad word.

A MAN who sells combs on the street left his shoes with Rafaniello and went away barefoot. He comes back to pick them up, sits down, and unwraps the dirty rags from around his feet. Rafaniello takes out the shoes. The man can't recognize them they look so new. He hugs Rafaniello, hump and all, giving him a big squeeze. It hurts Rafaniello because of the wings pressing on him from the inside. The comb seller brought along a basin.

He fills it with water and washes his dirt-caked feet, making them clean again out of respect for the pair of shoes perfumed with grease and polish. He does it for Rafaniello, who always recommends cleanliness. He wants to give him a comb made out of bone, but it would take a copper comb at the very least to straighten out the wild red mop on Rafaniello's head. He hugs and kisses him again and then leaves, singing out to Montedidio the cry of his trade that makes me laugh: *"Pièttene, pettenésse, pièttene larghe e stritte, ne' perucchiù, accattávene 'o pèttene,"* which sounds all right in Neapolitan, which is always happy to be insolent, but you wouldn't buy a hairpin from someone who went around saying in Italian, "Combs, combs, thick and thin, even you little nitpickers, buy yourself a comb." His voice is loud and from down the street we hear him cry, "Don Rafaniello the shoemaker is the master of all masters and even makes the lame walk."

~ ~ ~

OTHER POOR people don't make as much of a ruckus, but from their hoarse little voices come blessings as powerful as a cannon shot. Rafaniello answers, *"Mirzasè,"* which in his language means "if God wishes." No prince carries the blessings that you find in the bones of the poor, which start in their feet, run through their entire body, and spring from their mouths. The poor have a gratitude that no king has ever felt, and they push Rafaniello closer to Jerusalem. So he says, and I believe him. At lunchtime the workshop closes; Rafaniello takes off his jacket and asks me what I see on his hump. I see a cut, a purple spot on the top. It's starting to break, he says, like an eggshell. I slip the boomerang into the piece of string I sewed inside my jacket and climb the hill toward home.

~ ~ ~

I PASS the landlord on the stairs. I bite my tongue to avoid saying hello. He doesn't notice me. He's climbing fast, out of breath, goes past his own floor, goes to Maria's. I can see that he's carrying a box of pastries. For the first time I think of the boomerang I'm wearing as a weapon. I'd like to throw it at him. The wood turns heavy at the evil thought. I enter the house. It's empty, quiet. I open the windows and let in the autumn air, rotting on the southwest wind. Mama hasn't come back. Papa walks around the house without speaking. He doesn't come in to see if I'm in my room, if I'm asleep. We've grown apart. I put food on the table with the money he leaves me. On a piece of paper I write down what I spent and leave him the change. For now I'm holding on to my pay from Master Errico. I remember the verses Mama used to sing when she'd sit beside me for a minute after we'd said our bedtime prayers: *"Oi suonno vieni da lo monte / viènici palla d'oro e dàgli 'nfronte / e dàgli 'nfronte senza fargli male."* O sleep, come from the hills, come to us, golden moon, and strike him in the head, strike him in the face, but don't hurt him. The music would weigh upon my eyes and close them. Now I turn in without saying good night. Lying on my side, I send myself to sleep, as Rafaniello says when he goes to bed.

I STILL say my prayers. There's no window inside the closet where I sleep, so while I say my prayer to the Guardian Angel I imagine I'm up by the washbasins with the wide-open sky taking the place of the ceiling. I don't think I'm praying out of faith, just out of habit, so as not to lose the last words of the night. Rafaniello says that God is forced to exist by virtue of our insistence. By virtue of our prayers His ears are shaped, by virtue of our tears His eyes can see, by virtue of our joy His smile appears. Just like the boomerang, I think. By virtue of practice I prepare the throw, but can practice give rise to faith? I write down his words. Maybe later on I'll understand them. He says you should sing to air your thoughts, otherwise they'll grow moldy in your mouth. If I start singing with this cracked voice of mine, we'll be having a music festival in here! Master Errico wants to be heard over the sound of the planing machine. Don Rafaniè, I ask, you don't think that by virtue of staying in Naples you've become Neapolitan? No, he jokes, but the Neapolitans just might be one of the ten lost tribes of Israel. What? You lost ten tribes? So how many are left? "Just two. One of them is the tribe of Judah, whom the Jews are named after. It's a name that comes from the verb 'to thank.' " So the Jews are really named "thank you"? "That's what the word says, but all living people should be named this way, with a word of thanks."

～ ～ ～

TODAY IN the warm little sun of November the alleyway people leaned their heads out the windows, pushed their chairs in the street a little closer to the brazier. *"È asciuto, 'o pate d'e puverielle,"* says Master Errico. The father of the poor has come out. In the cold months the sun places its own blanket over the shoulders of those who don't have one. The voices of the street vendors rise in Montedidio, taking advantage of the open windows to call out their wares from the streets to the rooms. "Olives from Gaeta, I've got olives, sweet as rock candy, lower your baskets." Their shouts bring people to the windows. I couldn't keep my eyes off the street while I was working. It's not that I wanted olives. I wanted to go out. I'm learning that work is all about being good and doing your job while outside a low sun comes and goes in an instant. Evening falls and you're still cooped up in the shop. You saw the sun go by and didn't have a chance to greet it. Sing, Rafaniello says, thoughts need to be released, to find a way out. I nod in agreement, but not even broken breath comes out of my mouth. If I were outside, then maybe a song would break out, but only my eyes can go outside. The door is open. The sea breeze carries the smell of the docks all the way up here. I feel like I'm smelling my father's jacket, grease and salt, tar and rust. I forget my melancholy. Rather than sing, rather than sigh, I breathe in through my nose the sea air and the wind. The cries of the olive vendor come closer. I think of my father inside the hold of some ship and maybe he, too, feels like coming up for air. He deserves it more than I do. This is my first encounter with sadness.

IN SUMMER my mother used to take me outside the gate, where we waited for his shift to end. You never knew whether he would get out on time or have to stay and put in more hours. I'd be right outside, looking at the people on the Beverello pier getting on the white ferryboats of the Naples port authority. They were on their way to the islands, getting on and off board in straw hats. There was always someone who'd been scorched by the sun. Mama would laugh at how much they looked like tomatoes. *"Sbarcano 'e pummarole."* The tomatoes are landing! She never went sunbathing, never went to the beach. I've still never gotten on a ferryboat, but if I do I sure won't wear a straw hat. We would wait for Papa, and when he came out, fresh and clean with his hair slicked back, in his good jacket and a white shirt buttoned up to the collar, we were the best-looking family on the promenade. We would walk as far as Mergellina, passing by the Santa Lucia neighborhood. He would buy me a *tarallo* from Castellamare. Mama would give him her arm. I would be on his other side holding his open hand. People stepped aside so as not to disturb our formation. In Naples they respect families. When the paths of two families cross they say hello.

PAPA IS as tall as the wardrobe and just fits under the doorjamb. On the street he cuts quite a figure beside other men. Mama is tall, too, with dark black hair. She's skinny. In her face you can see her nerves. When a sudden gesture seizes her she's dangerous. She snaps like a spring, breaking the things around her. She bends her fork while she's eating if a thought makes her cross. I stopped giving her my hand when we went for walks. Sometimes she'd be lost in her thoughts and squeeze it so hard I would cry. Papa says she's stronger than him. On the promenade I don't think any child was prouder than me. Even in front of the sailing clubs where the gen-

tlemen with the money go, in the shadow of my two gi-
ants I felt like I had a fortune that no one could match.

WE USED to walk along the promenade by the Villa
Comunale when the shoreline fishermen were hauling
in the big net. There were six men to an end, all tugging
together. The oldest one kept time, shouting heave-ho.
The rope snaked from shoulder to shoulder, dragging
the sea into land. The net came closer, wide and slow,
while the two lines piled up in loops on the street.
When the net came in, the fish sparkled, their whiteness
leaping, flapping their tails by the hundreds, the net un-
loaded on dry land the pile of life stolen from the waves.
Papa would say, "Behold the flames of the sea." The
smell of the waterfront was our perfume. In the peace-
fulness of a summer day, when the sun was down, we'd

stand there wordlessly, close to each other. We used to do it until last year. Until last year I was still a child.

THE SMELL of the port has risen all the way to our alley, and I forget my sadness. Master Errico saw how far away I looked and told me to drink some octopus broth. *"Te magne 'a capa e metti giudizio";* eat one and it'll set your head straight. There's an octopus vendor at the top of the opposite alley. The only thing he sells is, *'e purpe.* Master Errico knows him, knows that he looks for octopus between the square stones of the outer breakwater. "He doesn't fish for them," he says. "He goes to pluck them out with his bare hands, like a breeder. He feeds them mussels. The octopus take comfort. He shucks the mussels, and the octopus come right up to him and eat out of his hands. He knows each and every one of them. He calls them by number. He wades into the water, says a number, and an octopus comes up and sticks to his hand. He kills them without hurting them, and the octopus that you get from him doesn't need to be tenderized. Even the big ones are already tender. He doesn't sell the little ones, the *purpetielli,* just the big ones. Go to him and drink the broth."

AT LUNCHTIME Rafaniello tells me stories about when he used to live in his hometown and was called Rav Daniel. When he was a boy he was apprenticed to a shoemaker, too. The shoemaker was mean, nothing like Master Errico. He didn't teach him the trade. Truth is, he hid everything from him. Rafaniello had to spy on him. The rest was taught to him in a dream by a shoemaker from the Holy Scriptures of his people. He would come at night and teach him the shoemaker's art. When Rafaniello was a boy he used to study after work, falling asleep on the open religious books. So it was easy for a saint to come out of the books to help him. The shoemaker in his dreams was named Rav Iohanàn has-sàndler, Master John the shoemaker, and he showed him the art that his boss wouldn't teach him. "I learned the shoemaker's trade in the Talmud," a big holy book from his hometown. Don Rafaniè, you even went to school in your sleep, you never get any rest. At night I can't figure anything out. Even if Fortune came by with the lottery numbers in her mouth, I'd tell her come back tomorrow. At night I don't exist for anyone. I sleep like a dead man. My eyes reopen at the same point where I closed them. Every morning is a resurrection.

WE SIT down on the shoe bench. He rubs his hump against the wall. I massage it a little for him. Under his jacket the bones are moving, the wing bones. We confide in each other. I tell him: Women give birth in the front, you're giving birth in the back. "Men don't have the honor of giving birth," he replies. We eat sitting close to each other. He rinses out his mouth and spits, like he does when he's about to say saintly things. "In my town I was reading the Psalms where you find the question, 'Who shall ascend into the hill of the Lord?' and the answer says, 'He that hath clean hands and a pure heart.' Then our area was struck by the war. It came from the west, crushing us, burning alive the land and the people. They were enemies I didn't know we had. I hid underneath animal dung, under a floor, in an abandoned limestone quarry. I resisted, without knowing why I wanted to live while everyone else was dying. I rebelled against dying and cursed it so I could live. I hid, ate, and drank all kinds of things, like boiled tree bark. I stole honey from beehives, drank my own urine mixed with snow. Job's wife tells him, 'Curse God and die.' But I didn't. Job didn't either. I didn't curse God and I'm not dead. The war cleansed my heart and washed my hands with lime. When it ended I was ready to ascend into the hill of the Lord."

~ ~ ~

HE TOLD me the rest of the story the next day, while outside it was raining. All the good clean water got wasted, running down to the sea without anyone putting out a kettle to catch some for pasta. Donna Speranza, the caretaker, collects the May rain. She says that it's good for the eyes. Rafaniello's tiny voice accompanies the water running down the alleyway. It's flowing, too. "Along with me, other people of my town emerged from their hiding places. They, too, had been rubbed with lime and made ready for the ascent. We headed south, descending toward Italy, a country that stretches far into the middle of the sea, so beautiful that it's a shame it ends and doesn't go farther. We try to embark for the land inscribed in our holy books. We have no passport, no rights, we are the living whom death has rejected. The English close off the sea. They don't let us go. I have an evil thought. 'You can keep your hill, keep your Englishmen in Jerusalem, make them your chosen people.' So He changes his mind. He takes away the English and plays a joke on me for punishment. He takes me to the mount of the Lord, but it's in Naples. It's true that here they know how to make perfect copies of antique furniture, luxury watches, and packs of American cigarettes. But copying the mount of the Lord is going too far. It can only be in Jerusalem. Here on top of the hill where you could see the sea and the peak of the volcano, you could fit a panoramic terrace, not the footstool for the feet of God. But they called it Montedidio, the hill of the Lord, and while they were at it, they called the hill next door Montecalvario, so that makes two," Rafaniello says, and he takes it for a joke, because you have to accept playful punishment, since sometimes God sets men straight by tricking them, that's what he says. "With all due respect, the Holy Land doesn't have franchises. In the meantime I've stayed here, on the slopes of another hill of the Lord, like a tourist who made the wrong booking." It must be because of his tiny voice. It must be the effort required to hear every word that makes me hear them again, as I write them, by ear, on the scroll of paper I keep in the evening, punctuated by the driving rain that keeps me away from the washbasins.

A FOREIGN shoemaker knows how to speak Italian so precisely that I'm moved, thinking of my dad who struggles to learn and doesn't know half as many words as Rafaniello. Did your Italian vocabulary come to you in dreams, too? I ask him. No, he says, he got it from books, reading *Pinocchio* over and over. I read it, too, I tell him, happy to have found something we've done together. He says that in his town Pinocchio would be named Iòsl and would be made out of wood, his whole life dedicated to his creator. "Now you know of my life as Rav Daniel and of the lives of the people from my town who are no longer here. Those who die leave history as a legacy to their children, to their relatives. My people left it to me and to some others. I'm telling you this because I'll be leaving before long, when this hump of bone and feathers finally cracks." Don Rafaniè, tell me about Jerusalem, about this place we can't copy. He cleans out his mouth, spits, then says that he still doesn't know, but someone told him, "In the city of Jerusalem, death is afraid of being swallowed by life. It's the only city in the world where death is ashamed of its existence." He closes his eyes, rocks his neck, he's already there. It must be a special place, Jerusalem. In Naples death isn't ashamed of anything.

RAFANIELLO LIKES garlic and oil, not tomato. From his bread with vegetables to my bread with anchovies, the lunch hour goes by. He says I've got secrets. He can read my mind, so I don't say anything. He asks how my mother is doing. I haven't seen her for a month. Papa doesn't want me to. He says she's under a tent with tubes attached and only he can go. To change the subject I say, you know, Don Rafaniè, you took the same journey as Saint Patricia. She wanted to go to Jerusalem, too, and a storm forced her to land in Naples. I tell him the story of the saint. She died young in Naples and left behind miraculous blood. It liquefies and solidifies all the time, even more than Saint Gennaro's blood. This gets Rafaniello's interest. Do you want to know how they got Saint Patricia's blood? One night a worshiper broke open her tomb and with a pair of pliers removed a tooth from the saint to keep as a relic. Though she had been dead for a hundred years, she started to spit blood from her gums. They collected it in glass jars and that's how the miracle was born. Don Rafaniè, things happen here that if you tell people about them, they think you're crazy, but they happen anyway. Naples is one big secret. "This is a city of blood," he says, "like Jerusalem." I know, I know, people are obsessed with blood here. They put it in their curses, in their insults. They even eat it cooked and then go to worship it in churches. Women are always going around saying, " 'O sang," bloody this and bloody that. Even the sauce we eat on Sundays is so dark, so thick, it looks like blood. Rafaniello is amused at the mysterious voice I'm using. Mysterious because it's hoarse.

AT THE washbasins Maria tells me that the old man came over with some pastries. Her mother went out to buy some coffee and he started up with his begging, saying that if she didn't come to him he'd die. "So I told him, go ahead, die. A lot of people younger than you die, you can die, too. His face turned from gray to red. He made like he was going to grab me. I ran around the table and he couldn't get me. 'You're mean,' he said, and started breathing so heavy he foamed at the mouth. Then he stopped, put a hand on his forehead, calmed down, and left. He left the pastries behind and we ate them." Maria says that he's dying, that he looked death in the face when she told him to die. All it takes is one word to wipe a man out. Maria knows a lot of things. For instance, she knows that she's stronger than an adult. I'm scared of adults. She isn't. She even attacks them. It must be because she's a girl and she's known disgust. She's thirteen and her breasts are growing faster than my boomerang muscles. She lets me touch them. They're firm. She says, "They're yours." My *piscitiello* gets hard and my mouth waters. She asks if I want her hands. I say no, Maria, don't do the same things to me you do to the old man. She says okay, you're right, we should make love, but she tells me in Neapolitan, *"Avimma fa' ammore,"* with two *m*s because that way it's tougher, more real. And I say we're already doing it. She says no, she means another kind, the kind where both of us are naked in bed like married people.

~ ~ ~

IT'S CHILLY at night by the washbasins. The clouds in the sky fan out like a fishbone. To feel warmer I practice harder, doing more turns. The Christmas month is at the door. During the day bagpipers come up to Montedidio. Maria brings a blanket to the roof. We sit on the ground and cover ourselves. When we're done talking, she pushes her mouth right on me. That's how we say good-bye. No good nights, no see you laters, no till tomorrows. Nothing. A kiss on the mouth and we're all right. I practice a little more. Right away the boomerang gets hot. The wood trembles, ready. It slices the air, pushes against the sky. I keep my feet far apart so I won't lose my balance when I start the release and suddenly stop short the flight of the boomerang. My right and left arms grow at the same rate, like Maria's breasts. The written part of the scroll gets longer. I don't read back. I can see that it's heavy. The part still to go is getting lighter. Maria doesn't know that writings about her are inside the scroll.

THE LANDLORD came by to pick up Master Errico's rent. Master Errico saw him coming and said, *"Vene chillo che tene."* The keeper is coming. He means that some men work and do things, and others just keep, they're owners and they don't do anything. The landlord doesn't say a thing. He's feeling low. He's got the blank look of someone who just got out of bed. Master Errico says nothing except, "good morning." He pays with the money he has ready. When the landlord leaves he says, "Something's eating the old man. Greedy as he is, this is the first time he hasn't counted out the money." I ask if he's really so greedy. "Greedy's not the word for it. He's got a virgin hand. No one has ever managed to pry his fingers open." For Maria's sake I added my own two cents, saying that he was an evil man. Master Errico immediately reprimanded me. "Listen, kid, talk behind someone's back and their ass will answer you." I was so embarrassed I slapped myself. Either say it to his face or keep quiet.

THE REST of the day I was thinking about Uncle Totò, whom I never knew. He was killed at noon one day in front of the main post office when an airplane dropped a bomb. Papa was his older brother. When he used to go down to the docks he would take Totò with him as far as the sidewalk on Via Medina, where Totò used to shine shoes. The bomb cut him in two. Papa ran from the docks after the bombing and found Totò at his usual spot. The shoeshine stand remained intact. My uncle was cut in two. It was July. There was dust all over the bodies of the dead and not a single fly. They were dead, too. This detail stuck in my father's mind and he repeats it whenever he wants to remember Uncle Totò. Every year Papa brings me with him to lay a flower on the common grave. The cemetery is a zoo for the dead. They're locked up inside. I went with Papa and Mama to the zoo one autumn day. We brought along stale bread. I gave some to the elephant, who took it from my hand with his trunk, so delicately it was like a caress. Papa was happy to hear me say the names of the stranger animals. There was some bread for the hippopotamus, too. I dropped a piece into its open mouth, which was as wide as a closet. Papa collected berries from the eucalyptus, a name he can't pronounce. He says *"calippeso."* He keeps them in his pocket. He likes the smell and sniffs at them when he's in the hold of the ship.

THE CAGES have names outside, animals inside, standing there. That's how they fight back, standing still and refusing to give us any satisfaction. Only the wolf keeps going in circles, out of homesickness and to get some exercise inside the cage. He stares off into the distance, even if there is no distance before him. He's running around waiting for a hunter, a savior, is what I think. The dead are caged animals, awaiting resurrection. Uncle Totò is a wolf, eager to run far away from Via Medina ever since the day they locked him up. I'm older than he ever was. His life ended before he was ten, one day short of his birthday. He never went to school. That's why Papa cares so much about education, so that I won't be held back by the street, so that I won't be stuck there.

~ ~ ~

NICE COOL evenings come, buffeted by the wind that ascends the Vomero and San Martino hills and passes over Montedidio before rubbing against the sea. I wait for Maria to come up to the terrace. I practice and look at the sky to find a target. I'll throw the boomerang, closing my good eye and opening up the bad one so that I can stare into the distance without crying. Later on, Maria and I scour the starry sky, our noses in the air. She says it's a lid; I say it's a fishnet, and every star's a knot. She says that we're the same height. Even those of us on the ground seem to float in the sky like buoys.

CHRISTMAS COMES. At Maria's house the creditors knock on the door and make a scene. On the stairwell you can hear the screaming. Her mother won't open up, her father's gone out. Papa comes home at six when I warm up his coffee. I drink some, too. He doesn't say a word. When Mama was around I used to drink coffee substitute. Now he wouldn't even notice if I started smoking. Grown-ups withdraw into their troubles and leave us behind in houses that don't make a sound. We only hear ourselves, which is a little scary. The spirits rub against my face in the empty kitchen and soothe me. The boomerang is always against my skin and it warms me. Its wood holds so much heat it must have been grown in a pan of sunlight. Maria bundles herself up against the cold with me and an overcoat. I'm upwind from her so I shield her. Christmas is coming, Maria says. Let's buy a chicken and cook it. Who needs them. It'll be the best Christmas of all. I'll bake some cookies, she says, and plants a kiss on my cold hair. The north wind rains kisses down upon me.

~ ~ ~

PAPA INFORMS me that on Christmas night he'll be in the hospital with Mama. This disease is something between them. My job is to take care of the house and wait. I'm waiting. For the flight of the boomerang. For it to break away after my shoulders have gone through the motions of throwing it and go hurtling off into the darkness, for it to smack against the stars, against what Maria calls the lid and I call the fishnet. I feel strong enough to throw it into the clouds. The boomerang is getting lighter, getting ready. It won't be long now. In the meantime Rafaniello is looking more like a bird. He's getting thin, the bones are poking through the skin of his face. Don Rafaniè, you've got to eat. Bread, oil, garlic, and onion aren't enough. The trip is long and you're traveling in winter. The other birds have already come and gone. I know, he replies. In his hometown in September he saw the storks join together in the sky to go to Africa. They pass near Jerusalem. "Inside my head the eye of a stork is breaking through to show me the way." When's it going to be? I ask. "When the wood of the Ark of the Covenant flies, that is what the angel told me. I'm keeping myself ready for the night of the end of the year. The Neapolitans throw old things out the window. Without realizing it, one of them's going to throw out a piece of the Ark." Then he adds, in a birdlike voice, "He'll throw it out because the Ark no longer holds the tablets of the Law, the Ten Commandments." He's right, I think. That night no one will notice Rafaniello's flight.

I'M STANDING there holding the broom, lost in thought, when Master Errico comes in early and says, "You're already here? What, you like the job?" Yes, I say, I eat with Don Rafaniello. Master Errico remembers that at home I haven't got anyone and invites me to his house for lunch to have some hot food. "Tomorrow I'm getting braided mozzarella from Agerola; have you ever tried it, kid? It's special. Agerola's high up. The cows there eat poplar leaves. Poplar leaves are what gives the cheese the bitter taste that makes it so special. Do you want to come?" I thank him, but things are all right the way they are. I'm happy to stay in the workshop at lunchtime. "Suit yourself, I'm not going to tell you where to vote," he says. Master Errico lights his half-smoked cigar and starts up the bench saw. The most he and Rafaniello do is exchange greetings, but they do it properly, purposefully. They respect each other. "Don Rafaniello's made shoes for all Montedidio. Before, everyone used to go barefoot." "And you gave me wood to keep warm and a place to sleep. Without you I would have gotten lost in the alleyways by the port." "With that mop of red hair on your head you couldn't get lost in *'na sporta 'e purtualle,*" in a basketful of or-anges, I translate for him.

~ ~ ~

AT THE workshop Master Errico reads in the newspaper about the man who's nicknamed The Jinx. One day out of desperation he decides to throw himself from a window and ends up falling on top of some unlucky guy who was passing by that very spot. The passerby dies, and The Jinx breaks two ribs. "Check out the numbers, kid," he says. "You should play them on the lottery." In the meantime he goes over to rub the red horn hanging in the doorway to the workshop. Rafaniello mumbles a spell in his language and spits on the ground. We never let superstition into the house. Papa says it's for women. Mama says it's a bunch of nonsense and that men are more obsessed by it than women. Master Errico says we're alive by accident and scrape along by hiding from God. All it takes is one dirty look and we're done for. Around here no one would ever say "Lucky you" to someone else. People would immediately call you a jinx if something bad happened to the other guy. A man twists his ankle and blames it on the person who wished him good luck. Rafaniello says that in his hometown they say *"anóre"* for evil eye. He remembers that his mother was beautiful. They even paid her compliments when she was pregnant, and she kept them for herself, she didn't do anything to exercise the bad luck they bring. That's why her son was born a hunchback. At home they scolded her. If she had only said *"cananóre,"* her son would have been born healthy. Nothing causes more damage than an envious eye, Master Errico says.

DON LIBORIO is scared of good-luck wishes, too. For the mid-August holidays he closes his print shop and goes up to the Matese mountains to breathe the air. While loading his suitcase into the taxi on his way to the bus, he runs into Don Ferdinando, the undertaker, who sends him customers for death notices and is also a good friend. He sees the suitcase and says, "Don Libò, have a good trip," and Don Liborio answers, "Thanks, but I'm not leaving, I just arrived," and takes his suitcase out of the taxi and goes back home. He left the next day instead. He told the story to Master Errico, who noticed that the print shop was open that evening and wondered why he was still in the city. "What else could I do? How was I supposed to leave with the greetings of the gravedigger?" Then Master Errico put aside the newspaper and ended the talk with a carpenter's spell. "Saint Joseph, *passace 'a chianozza*"—pass over this talk with a planer.

I TOLD Rafaniello about Maria and the landlord. He stayed quiet for a while, then closed his eyes tight and said, "May you share the fate of the dog who licks the rasp." His voice was as cold as the north wind. I felt a shiver in my kidneys. What are you saying Don Rafaniè? "A curse," he answered, but with his own voice again. "I'm saying it, but it's not mine. It comes through me, into the open. Your story has been heard. That man has been struck by a pellet of hail." There are many things I don't understand, including the part about the dog. Don Rafaniè, is it bad that curse about the dog? "It's bad. The dog licking the rasp is licking his own blood, but his liking for blood is greater than the pain, so he keeps licking till he bleeds to death." Night has fallen. It's time to close up. I've finished my cleaning so I give Rafaniello a hand straightening out his bench. The sound of bones comes from his hump. He looks up, pushing back the bag with the wings. His round green eyes search the sky for a spot to climb. The city rises upward in walls and balconies. There is no sky overhead. But he finds a way to get his bearings even in this canyon. His head has the same compass as a stork. I roll the gates down and we say good night. He says it's nice to have wings, but it's nicer to have good hands for work.

MASTER ERRICO sets the alley spinning with his voice. He's furious. He's showing his ugly side. A workman was fixing a cornice on a top-floor balcony. All at once there was a crash in the alley. Master Errico ran out and saw the rubble. He started screaming at the workman that downstairs there were children, people. The guy answered that he had work to do, so Master Errico let his animal out and shouted, *"Scinne!"* Get down here! Get down here and go home while you've still got legs to walk on. Otherwise I'll come up and break them. He said it in Neapolitan so loud that the whole alley quieted down. The workman saw that the day was taking a turn for the worse and came down. Everyone was looking out the windows and doors and Master Errico stood in the middle of the alley. I came out to sweep up the rubble. "Stand back," he said. "That guy's got to do it." Things were getting serious. "Don't pay attention to him, Mast'Errì, don't get all worked up, let the boy do it." The voice of Don Liborio the typographer calmed Master Errico down. "Come on, let's have a coffee." He took his arm and led him up the street. I swept up the rubble and the workman was able to leave.

THE WOMEN were talking, saying that he had done the right thing. The women in Naples are always egging on the men. The oldest one said that Master Errico was a real kingpin, and during the September uprising against the Germans he got the whole block together to drive them out of Naples. Another woman said that when there's someone like Master Errico on the block the criminals are nowhere to be found. The women talked, so I learned about past events. Back in those days my father was at the port defending his job. The people of Naples went wild. They took to the streets yelling, *"Iatevenne!"*—get out of here! and they used guns to show the Germans to the door. Some even lost their lives. So this afternoon I asked Master Errico about it. He answered that everyone had come out that day—Don Liborio, Don Ciccio the doorman, the women, the street urchins, the city's whole motley crew. "The Germans were tearing everything apart, dropping bombs on houses. In the end they wanted to take all of the young men to Germany to work for them. Anyone who didn't report was shot. The only ones on the streets were old people and women. We wanted to drive them out. We didn't want to hide anymore. The Americans showed no signs of entering Naples. They were waiting. So we got sick of waiting."

~ ~ ~

I WANTED to hear more. After I pestered him for a while with questions, he continued. Master Errico was in the right mood. "Even Father Petrella the priest got involved. During the bombardments he had learned to say mass quickly, fifteen minutes at most. The practice has stayed with him, which is why they call him Father Fast. Once an air-raid siren went off after Communion, just as he was finishing the service. Rather than say the usual, *'Ite, missa est,'* he said, *'Fuite!'*—make a run for it—*'missa est!'* He was the first to run like a hare, blessing the shelter while he was running and holding up his cassock, the landlord close on his heels, followed by retired General De'Frunillis. During the September uprising even Don Petrella came into the line of fire, not to hurt the Germans but to bring us comfort. He gave absolution to those who were dying from gunshot wounds, including a German soldier. The whole neighborhood came out. When it was over, I said, 'Now this city is mine.' " Rafaniello listened with tears in his eyes.

PAPA SPOKE with me. They've got some hope for Mama. Sitting down to coffee at six in the morning while the block is silent and dark, he lays it out for me. This year there will be no Christmas. "The only thing I care about is her, and she is leaning on me with all the strength she has left. She's weak, but not her hands. She squeezes tight. She even broke a glass and cut herself. We're fighting this one together. We don't want to put you in the middle. It's between us, going back to when we went to the air-raid shelters during the bombings and swore that we would never be apart, bombs or no bombs. No one could separate us. When a bomb exploded nearby, the blast made her throw up. I held her head and she vomited between my feet. I was happy that our love could do even this. We were engaged back then and even closer than newlyweds. The war allowed us to be the way we are. If she leaves, I'll be like a doorknob without a door." He forced himself to use Italian. He wanted to speak with me. He made me feel important. I didn't say anything. I looked him right in the face. It was a small thing, to stay right in front of him and listen as well as I could, keeping my eyes on him and not moving. Then he let out what he was thinking. "All three of us will get back together, as if nothing happened, we'll go back to having our Sundays. Do you remember the Solfatara Volcano?" It was time to go. That's where he stopped. He got up and rinsed his cup out in the sink. It was the first time he'd done it. He splashed some water on himself, dried off, and smiled at me.

~ ~ ~

HE WAS really confiding in me. He explained carefully, mustering the patience he needed to speak Italian. In his mouth it becomes a Sunday language. When he can't find a word he turns red from the effort and I find it for him. Right away he says, "Bravo," and repeats what I said, even if it isn't the word he was looking for. Yes, I'm thinking of the Sunday we saw the Solfatara Volcano. "You're thinking about it, aren't you? *'A tieni mente?*" Yes, it's fresh in my mind. He wants to climb Vesuvius, too, on a winter Sunday when there's snow on top. "Do you remember the snow?" he asks me sometimes, and I nod yes, and stare out into the darkness. I can see the 1956 snowstorm, the soft rain of the north, white and silent. We tell each other about it again and every winter he tells me, "This year it's going to snow by the sea, too," out of his desire to see it again. The port becomes clean. You can't see the dirt, the oil, the rust. Silence grips the city. Even the streetcar forgets that it's made of steel and passes by as quietly as a trolley bus. "Even the garbage piles, *'e muntune 'e munnezza,* seem beautiful." The oak trees at the Villa Comunale wear white skullcaps and I wonder: How do the blind get by without white?

PAPA LEFT with a change of clothes for Mama, wrapped up in a paper bundle under his arm. I turn the light off. I'm alone. It's cold. I squeeze the boomerang in my hand and warm myself. Of course I remember the Solfatara Volcano in Pozzuoli, Papa. You took me there one Sunday, without Mama, who couldn't stand the stench and doesn't wear perfume. We took the streetcar as far as Bagnoli, then went the rest of the way on foot. It was drizzling, raindrops as fine as pinheads tickling the calm sea and the tar-mottled beach. Under the umbrella I walked at your pace. I had to rush. I didn't pay attention to the puddles and my feet got wet. Outside the entrance the air was already heavy with sulfur. We went in, Papa, and you started reading one of the signs out loud: *The* solfatara *is a volcanic exaltation.* The right word was *exhalation*, but I didn't correct you. When a volcano dies, it exhales its final warmth in green brimstone salts the same color as Rafaniello's eyes. We arrive at the crater, which is sunken into the plain. A silent smoke rises from the crusts of earth. A pond of mud boils, bubbling on the surface. Papa closes the umbrella. The steam from the *solfatara* stops the rain. The only sound is of shoes touching the ground. With no city movement around me I feel a little dizzy.

I SEE a black butterfly. I read the names written below the plants near the crater: laurel, myrtle, arbutus. At one fumarole I remove my shoes and let my trousers dry. The earth is hot. It feels good on my back. A smell of burning rises from the bottom of my trousers. Too late I realize that the seat of my pants is scorched. Papa laughs, but he stops when he realizes that Mama will have to fix them. We circle the crater. I pick up green stones that are good for writing, like chalk at school. I think I still have them somewhere. If I find them I'll bring them to Rafaniello to see if they match his eyes. On the way back Papa buys Mama a cut of *musso*, boiled calf's lip. That's how we are going to apologize for the trousers. Then we go up the hill to Montedidio. The students of the Nunziatella Military Academy pass us in their gold-buttoned uniforms, with white-handled dress swords hanging from their belts. Their clothing glares next to the shabby clothing of the crowds around them. They're kids, a few years older than me, walking with their chests out and not looking anyone in the face. It must be awful to set yourself apart from other people that way, shunning them. At home Mama didn't say a thing about the trousers or the *musso,* no scolding and no thanks. So we're even.

~ ~ ~

RAFANIELLO'S FACE is all crumpled. He didn't sleep. The wings broke through the shell of his hump. It cracked like an egg, without bleeding. His jacket's gotten fuller. He says he's managed to open the wings. They're bigger than a stork's. He's decided to wait for the night of fireworks. In the meantime he's practicing in his room at night. The fireworks in Naples used to scare him, reminding him of the turmoil of war. "This time they'll be bidding me farewell." I tell him that I've made my decision, too. I'm going to throw the boomerang the same night. The boomerang's wings are ready, too. "How much time do we have left?" he asks. Two weeks. From my pocket I take one of the brimstones. It's the same color as your eyes, I say. He holds it up against the light. "Fire and brimstone. It rained fire and brimstone on Sodom and Gomorrah. Green eyes, red hair. The Heavenly Father made me look like an ember." I wonder if his eyes are really green. What's more, I say, they're lit like teardrops, not brimstone. Rafaniello is getting to the bottom of his shoe pile. People have been coming by to pick them up. He's not accepting broken ones anymore. Now everyone's wearing shoes in Naples.

I HELP Master Errico plane some larch boards. They give off a scent of resin, a smell that clears your sinuses. Master Errico looks at the first planing and shakes his head. "We can't use the machine," he says. "We have to finish it by hand." He shows me the drops of resin and says that they're hard and would break the blade of the planing machine. Larch resin dries as hard as a rock. So I learn to move the hand planer, following Master Errico. The larch shavings are blond and not very curly. It's like giving the wood a crew cut. At noon I realize that a feather has fallen under Rafaniello's bench. I pick it up. It's so light I can't feel it in my palm. Don Rafaniè, I'm going to hold on to this to remember you by. "You're right to say 'hold on to' instead of 'keep.' To keep is presumptuous. To hold means you realize that today it's yours and tomorrow who knows. Hold on to the feather as a keepsake." I think of the boomerang. I hold it tight, then I have to let it go. I take it out of my smock. Look at it, Don Rafaniè, it's so well made that it can fly, too. We chew our bread and *friarelli* and stare at the boomerang. He stops eating and asks me very seriously what kind of wood it's made from. Acacia, Don Rafaniè, a hardwood. His breath catches in his throat. He coughs loud and spits up some *friarello,* then he calms down and rocks back and forth in his chair, repeating, "Acacia, acacia," with tears in his eyes, his face as red as his hair, a crunching of bones behind his back.

~ ~ ~

As I write this on my scroll I can't remember how to say it in Italian: did he break out in tears or did the tears break out? Who could tell at noontime? I didn't and couldn't understand a thing. I waited next to him without eating. I didn't look at him. I waited. He finally managed to clear his throat and make a different sound, more like laughter, a laughter more silent than the tears that had come before. He laughed and made me laugh just to see how it cracked him up to repeat the word *acacia,* strangling the sound of the *a* and laughing, laughing hysterically, and I laugh with him, thinking that if Master Errico were to come in now and find us like this, he'd throw a bucket of cold water over us to make us stop. Rafaniello calms down and I'm happy since the laughter gave me back my appetite. I finish my bread and *friarelli* in four bites. I arrange the boomerang under my jacket near the feather that fell from Rafaniello's wings.

~ ~ ~

AT THE washbasins in December the wind gets all blustery, sweeping up the dirt on the ground, polishing the nighttime sky, drawing off the heat from the houses. The boomerang is going wild. It burns the air that will carry it on its flight. My arms can't control it. It's like a wing with feathers. I wind myself up to toss it two hundred times with one arm, two hundred with the other, and I don't get tired. I'm a thrower and have to force myself to wait. There's the dark side of the moon. Maria stares at the giant lid over Montedidio, spellbound. I'm obsessed with the sea and think all the shiny points on its surface are a school of anchovies. With my broken voice I imitate the cry of the fishmonger when he comes by with a basket on his head and a scale around his neck calling out: " 'O ppane d'o mare"; bread of the sea. "Quiet, you're making me think of the smell of fish," says Maria, who can't stand fish and would just as soon leave it in the sea. On the highest rooftop in the neighborhood she and I are keeping watch over the city. Sitting close to the ground against the bulwark, covered by the blanket, we pass the time, accomplices of the wind that mocks the television antennas and empty clotheslines. It whistles overhead, discovers our shelter, and gives us a push to bring us closer together.

MARIA HUGS me, leaning her head against my neck. We speak to each other in whispers. She says, "You get bigger every day and I'm holding on to you so that I can grow quickly, too. Only yesterday you didn't have these muscles on your chest. Only yesterday you weren't so right for me." I don't know about yesterday. Today's already gone by, planed into the blond shavings of larchwood, the shape of the planer indented in my palm. And only toward the end of the day does my hand return to its place around the boomerang and around Maria's shoulders. Yesterday is the part of the scroll that's already been written on and rolled up. Maria, I ask, is this the *ammore* they talk about in songs? "No," she says, "love songs are too gloomy, a lot of sloppy weeping and teardrops. Our *ammore* is an alliance, a combat force." Our intimate talk flies into the wind, which tears it from our mouths.

IN THE dark we can make out the figure of a person on the roof buffeted about by the wind, calling out Maria, Maria. It's the landlord. She goes tense beside me and doesn't answer. I slip out of the blanket. I grab the old man by the lapels with the force of the boomerang in my arms and push him away. He keeps calling Maria and bumps into me as if I were the wind, as if he couldn't see. He's coming back this way, says Maria. Without a word I bounce him off my hands which are getting stronger and stronger. The boomerang under my jacket pushes him, too. The wind grabs me by my shoulders and sends me hurtling into him. I move him backward with a jolt, and beaten back, he staggers forward. I'm ready for him again and I pick him up like the arc of the boomerang. I don't see his face. I look as far as his jacket and aim for his chest. With the last push I slam him against the door to the stairway, which opens up behind him. He realizes there's nothing left to do, doubles over in pain from the blows to his chest, from Maria, I don't know, he doubles over, sits down, and cries. I see a defeated old man, beaten outside and in, and still I feel no pity. I go back to Maria, who's standing up. She puts her cold arms around me and forces a frosty kiss inside my mouth, tooth to tooth. Her shivering begins to pass.

~ ~ ~

THE OLD man is a goner. He's got the curse of the dog that licks the rasp. I saw him crying, Maria. "I saw him crying, too, between my legs." We gather up the blanket, leave the roof, shut out the wind behind our backs. She says, "You've gotten rid of him forever." Away from the open air her voice rings out harshly in the stairwell. On Christmas Eve, she says, we'll stay together at your house and have our own party without any adults, just us two allies. All right, I say, with my pay from Mast'Errico I'll buy the capon and the potatoes. "I'll make cookies and get all dressed up." I open her door with the keys, go downstairs, pass in front of the landlord's apartment. My hands are still burning. I notice a button that got caught in my sleeve and drop it on the ground in front of his door.

~ ~ ~

WHILE MASTER Errico is counting out my week's pay in my hand, he asks if my mother is feeling better, if she'll be home for Christmas. I shake my head no. "So, you won't be having eel?" No, Master Errico, eel's too difficult. It even slithers away after it's been cut. I'm buying capon. I ask him if he's going fishing tomorrow. "Depends on the weather." Then Rafaniello tells me to never ask a fisherman whether he's going out. They guard their plans jealously. If they talk about them it brings bad luck. It's only afterward that they talk about the fish they caught. Rafaniello knows Neapolitan. He says it resembles his native language. To him Italian's like a piece of fabric, a garment draped over the naked body of dialect. He adds, "Italian is a language without saliva. But Neapolitan's got spit in its mouth that helps you stick your words together. Stuck with spit: for the sole of a shoe it's no good, but it makes a good glue for dialect. In my language we say the same thing: *zigheclèpt mit shpàiecz;* glued with spit." He makes me repeat it so I can write it on the scroll. I ask him what he's doing on Christmas Eve. He's not doing anything. He's not a Christian. I invite him over. I tell him I'll cook capon, without saying a thing about Maria. He thanks me, his smile wrinkling his skinny face. The fresh green of his eyes sparkles among his red freckles. His smile breaks to respond to the invitation by saying no.

I CLOSE the workshop an hour early, a little before the stores close, and go out to look for capon at the butcher's and potatoes at the vegetable pushcart. "All of Naples is in the street," says the washerwoman, leaning out the window of her ground-floor apartment. She brought in the clothes on the line. The crowd was banging into them, getting them dirty. *"Simme assaie, nuie simme tropp'assaie."* Too many of us, way too many of us, says De Rogatis, the music teacher, waiting in line outside the fish shop for them to wrap his live eel. "I want to pick my own," one woman protests to the fishmonger. "They're all the same, ma'am," he shouts back, holding the slithering thing by its head. A woman drove down the alley in a car and hit Don Gaetano the tailor, who was sitting on a stool on the curb, mending a pair of trousers by the light of the street lamp to save on electricity. She ran into him and the stool, sending them rolling down the street. There were shouts, the woman fainted, everyone rushed over to give her a hand. Don Gaetano was left on the ground, in a daze. He still didn't know what had hit him and kept asking, "What happened?" In this crowd you don't feel the cold. It's better than a coat. At the door Donna Speranza the caretaker is the first to greet me, "Merry Christmas, kid." An even better one to you, Donna Speranza, I answer, and show her the beautiful capon I bought.

~ ~ ~

I ENTER the house. A cold so still and silent you want
to jump into bed. I sprinkle salt and pepper on the capon and put it in the oven with the potatoes. A blast
of heat. In the kitchen I can hear the radio from the
house across the way. On Via Santa Maria della Neve
an elderly woman went out in the street and threw into
the air all the coins she had collected from panhandling.
A crowd gathered and the police intervened. The blood
of Saint Andrew of Avellino liquefied. Far from Naples,
in America, they made a young man president. The
Russians sent a dog up in a rocket. The Americans sent
a monkey instead. I turn off the lights and look outside.
It's Christmas. Rooms are lit and families are sitting
down at the table. On the table I've set places for the
boomerang, the capon, and Maria with her cookies. In
the past year I never dreamed of asking so much. It hap-

pened by itself, without my wishing it. My grown-up body, Maria's mouth, Rafaniello's wings. So much abundance arrived without asking, except for Christmas. With the lights out I feel the spirits caressing my neck. They move about better in the dark. I use the light of the street lamp to write, leaning against the railing of the balcony. The sound of my pencil on paper captures the noises of the day.

WHEN SHE knocks on the door I put away my scroll and turn on the lights. In she comes, wearing a red dress, perfume, and carrying cookies fresh from the oven. "Tonight we're going to make love," she says, "*facimmo ammore.*" I've cooked capon, I tell her, with new potatoes. She lets her nose lead her to the kitchen and pushes me in the same direction. The room is dark.

Maria places her arms around me from behind. She holds me tight, doesn't turn me around. She plants kisses on the back of my neck, the same spot where you grab a puppy, she tickles me, I hold in my laughter. Then she kisses my throat. It tickles inside. The scent of her perfume enters my nostrils. It smells like a Christmas tree, stronger than the smell of the capon in the oven. My mouth waters. I'm embarrassed that while she's kissing me all over my body I'm standing there swallowing and don't even have an appetite. Where is the water in my mouth coming from? Maria holds me from behind and moves her hands up and down my sides. She moves them from my face to my throat, to my chest, and lower, where I don't dare to look. I keep swallowing, hoping she won't notice. She's breathing heavily, squeezing, unleashing her beautiful force on my body, laying the freshness of her hands on the hardened muscles that grow tense as they wait to respond to her.

~ ~ ~

SHE SAYS, "You're so strong." She keeps her arms around me and rubs her face against my back. Then she turns me around and presses me up against the wall. I bang into a skillet that's hanging there; she laughs, pushes me. Now I can embrace her, too. She's washed her hair. It falls on my face, like fresh clothes on the line, dark and loose. Her hands hold my face and press kisses against my open mouth. I don't know what to do with my hands. I try to break away from her a little and I place them on her breasts. Then I rub her. She gets warm and then just like that we take off our clothes and are naked on the kitchen floor and I have just enough time to turn the oven off so the capon won't burn. Maria leads, I follow. She positions me on top of her where she wants me, and I realize that I don't know where my *piscitiello* is. She's got it and is rubbing it between her legs. I can't reach it. I let her lead me. She lifts me up and lowers me, making a wave. I open my eyes and see her closed eyes below me, her mouth open, her dark hair scattered all around and the wave tosses, and I try to stay balanced, what an effort it takes to squeeze and hold, this is what beauty must be, then I feel a bolt unleashed from the top of my body, as if the boomerang were rushing out of my *piscitiello,* an "oof" of amazement comes out of me, she grabs my back even tighter and gives off soft short breaths into my ear and I make movements that don't belong to me.

MARIA SLOWLY comes to a stop. I've tired her, I've hurt her, I don't know. What did we just do, Marì? "We made love," she says. So this is love? This is what you taught me? "No," she says, "I don't teach you. I just start, you do the rest." Making love must be mysterious, it happens by itself, I think. In the meantime my *piscitiello* is back in its usual place. *"Arò si' gghiuto?"* Where did you go? I feel like asking it in Neapolitan, but I don't. "Now I feel better about all those times that this disgusted me," Maria says in a small voice, without all the usual toughness in her words. She's gotten hungry. We get up from the floor and put our clothes back on. She fixes her hair; I keep the light off. The kitchen has a little heat from the oven and we're still warm with love. We serve the capon with potatoes, sitting close to each other, side by side. We eat with our hands, bumping our elbows into each other, then we look and laugh at each other in the dark catching light from outside. We put our napkins around our necks, a few burps escape our lips, the boomerang is at the table with us. She puts the new potatoes in my mouth, I pretend I'm choking, we sop the bottom of the pan with our bread.

"IT'S NICE to be just the two of us and no one else," Maria says with her mouth full. Our eyes have gotten used to the dark. We put a blanket over our shoulders and eat the almond cookies. She made a lot and we eat them all. None are left over. "Next time I'm going to make a pie," she says. In the meantime, from the house next door, bagpipers start to play a song. The family invited them up to make a little music. We can hear it clearly. It must be so loud in their house that they have to cover their ears. We rub our messy mouths together and lick each other like cats. Later on we get into bed, my little bed in the closet. We fall asleep wrapped around each other so tight that whoever wakes first will have to wake the other to get free. Our bodies are tied in a knot.

DON CICCIO the caretaker was speaking with a tenant, saying that last night the landlord went crazy, knocking at the door to Maria's house for an hour. The neighbors woke up and got into a fight with him. On the second floor we didn't hear a thing. Even though it's Christmas I'm going to the workshop to open it anyway. Painted furniture dries better in the air. Rafaniello arrives after me and starts to work at his bench. The wings are filling out his jacket, bigger than his hump. How do they stay closed up in there? No one notices, no one catches it with their eyes. Master Errico can tell straight away if a sharp corner is off square by even a millimeter, but he wouldn't even look up if Rafaniello walked in one day without his hump. We're alone in the workshop. It's a nice day and Master Errico's gone off fishing for sure. Rafaniello asks me how the boomerang is doing. I take it out of my jacket and give it to him. He pretends to sniff it and then kisses it. I look, but I say nothing. Both the wood and Rafaniello have gotten lighter.

I PUT the furniture outside. Donna Assunta the washerwoman opens her ground-floor apartment and starts hanging out the wash. This morning there aren't many people about. The sun is out and they'll dry quickly. Good morning, I tell her. She asks how it is that we're open for Christmas. The furniture has to dry, too, Donna Assù, not just the clothes, I answer. She went to midnight mass. Father Petrella gave a nice sermon. He said that the rockets being shot into space go no-where. They get lost in the sky. But the comet came close to Earth to announce the birth of the infant, the *bambeniello*. "More than this, what more could we pos-sibly want from the stars? He spoke well, kid, quickly quickly, like he always does, but really well, and you should come to church. You don't want to grow up like some hoodlum. The last apprentice that worked for Master Errico never went to mass and now he's at the Poggioreale prison. Be smart, kid," Donna Assunta says, pinning the clothes to a line half as long as the alley with her chapped red hands. I nod yes with my head. She tries to think of the right words for me. Then she walks away and I mutter a spell to keep me out of

Poggioreale: *"Sciòsciò, sciòsciò."* I also say *"cananóre,"* which I just learned.

I SPEAK with Rafaniello. Today we've got the time. Don't you ever miss your hometown? I ask. His hometown doesn't exist anymore. Neither the living nor the dead remain, they made all of them disappear. "I don't miss it," he says. "I feel its presence. In my thoughts and when I sing, when I fix a shoe, I feel the presence of my hometown. It comes to visit me all the time, now that it doesn't have a place of its own. In the cries of the waterman ascending Montedidio with his cart to sell sulfur water in earthenware jars. I can hear a few syllables from my hometown even in his voice." He quiets down for a while with nails in his mouth and his head bent over the sole of a shoe. He sees that I've stayed near him and continues: "When you get homesick, it's not something missing, it's something present, a visit. People and places from far away arrive and keep you company for a while." So when I start feeling like I miss someone I should think that they're present instead? "Exactly, that way you'll remember to greet every absence and welcome it in." So when you've flown away I shouldn't miss you? "No," he says, "when you start to think of me it'll mean that I'm with you." I write down what Rafaniello said about homesickness on the scroll and now it's better. His way with thoughts is like his way with shoes. He turns them upside down on his bench and fixes them.

PAPA CAME home to change his shirt and found Maria there. She told him that she was there to straighten up the house and give me a hand. He thanked her, got a change of clothes for Mama, and left. He came by the shop to see me and didn't say a word about Maria. His eyes were glazed from fatigue. I don't ask, he doesn't say. His alliance with her is tighter and I'm not included. My alliance with Maria shuts us off from the world, too. Change happens, but especially to us. Who else has a face as crumpled as Papa's? Who else has a hump that's sprouting wings? Who else has a body ready to throw a boomerang? And now, of all times, Maria has broken away from an old man's filthy hands and been held by my hands, smoothed by sawdust, on the highest rooftop in Montedidio. When the fishnet gets closer to shore it starts to weigh less and can be pulled in more quickly. The same thing is happening to us. Even the scroll is winding up more quickly, drawn in by the weight of what's already been written.

I TAKE Rafaniello with me to the rooftop where the washbasins are. He hobbles up the stairs. He doesn't know how to walk. He leans over the bulwark, looking south and east. He opens the whites of his eyes, making the green circle pop out. It's not long now before we'll be saying good-bye. I ask him what he's thinking. It's noontime on Christmas. Everyone's at home. We're the only ones outside and the sea air is shining. Staring out without looking at me, he says, "We have a proverb that says, 'This is the sky and this is the earth,' to indicate two opposite points. Up here they're close together." You're right, Don Rafaniè, if you jump off the top of Montedidio you're already in the sky. "It'll take a few jumps and a big push. When you fly in your dreams you're weightless. You don't have to convince your strength to keep you up high. But when you add in the wings and the body, you have to be prepared to climb the air. You need something powerful to blast you away from Earth. I'm a shoemaker, a *sándler,* they used to say in my hometown. I fix shoes, I know feet, I know how they're supported, how they manage to balance the whole body towering over them. I know how useful the arches are, the hardness of the heel, the spring inside the anklebone that accompanies long jumps, wide jumps, high jumps. I know the suffering of the feet and the pleasure of being able to stand on any kind of surface, even a tightrope. Once I made a pair of buckskin shoes for a tightrope walker in the circus. Here in Naples I've learned that feet know how to sail. I've repaired shoes for sailors who have to withstand the rising and falling pendulum of the sea. Feet brought me as far as Montedidio, they saved me. My people say that the wolf's got something to eat thanks to its feet, not its teeth. I even have a hump that weighs down on me, so what is such an earthbound creature doing, flapping his wings in the sky below the stars?"

I WRITE his words to hear them again, not to remember them. I close my good eye, and while I write on the scroll in a crooked scrawl the voice of Rafaniello rustles again, together with the rustling of the spirits. "Wings are good for an angel, heavy for a man. The only thing a man needs to fly is prayer. Prayer climbs above clouds and rain, ceilings and trees. To fly is a prayer. I was crooked, a bent nail, twisted toward the earth. But another force turns me around and pushes me upward. Now I have wings, but to fly you have to be born from an egg and not from a womb, hatched in a tree, not on the ground." He leans over the bulwark, his wings beating against his jacket, I can't help but reach out to stop him. When I touch him he turns around and steps back down. His whole face is smiling but not his eyes. They are the eyes of a bird, motionless, lost in the middle of his face. Underneath my jacket the boomerang grows warm. I pat it approvingly.

As we go downstairs the sound of smashing plates comes from the landlord's apartment. Rafaniello stops and without knowing who lives in the house says, "This man is drunk on his own blood." Is that the curse of the dog, Don Rafaniè? He says yes and a cold jolt passes through my kidneys. I was the one who pushed him away from the roof toward the stairs. I struck him with open hands. I drove him away, I deserve to feel a chill in my back. I climb down the stairs after Rafaniello while the sound of smashing plates continues. Maria's at my house wearing an apron. She's waiting for me to return. She's preparing a sauce with onions. Her eyes are swimming in tears. She laughs. Don Ciccio the caretaker knocks on the door. We show him into the kitchen. He sits down with us and starts to speak. "Your families are falling apart and you two have gotten together. You're still children but you're doing the right thing. You have to help yourself. Here in Naples you grow up quickly."

DON CICCIO speaks softly, with his hands together on the table and his beret on his head, even indoors. "I've known you and Maria since you were in diapers, I know what you've been through." Maria stares at him, breathing hard through her nose, a sign of anger. "Marì, if at home there's no one to protect you and they get you in trouble instead, then no one can help you. The same thing happened in my family. It was wartime, there wasn't enough to eat, my little sister went up to that apartment and put bread on our table. Marì, don't look at me like that. Don't get all worked up if I tell you that I know what you went through. Now you have this boy here. A good boy, hardworking, he respects his elders, even confides in that foreign shoemaker, Don Rafaniello the hunchback, with that hump on his back as big as he is. You're right to be together. But do the right thing. Don't rush, you can't get married or live in the same house yet. Start off by getting engaged. Let other people know your intentions, otherwise you'll cause a scandal and your parents will have to step in. Even if right now they don't know you're alive, when people start talking they'll turn against you. I'm telling you this because I like you and you're doing the right thing, Marì, I'm glad that you're not going up to that apartment anymore." Don Ciccio said the last words with a catch in his throat and his face turned red.

IN SPRING I was still a child and now I'm in the middle of things I can't understand. Don Ciccio is right. Here you have to grow up quickly, and I do, I run. Rafaniello, Maria, the boomerang, I chase after them, in the meantime the scroll is winding up, all written, and I'm not going to Don Liborio to look for another leftover roll. Maria is seated across from Don Ciccio and doesn't say a thing. In the pot the sauce is simmering on a low flame. She takes my hand from under the table and puts it on the napkin together with hers. I look at her but she looks at Don Ciccio. "Now you tell me, Don Ciccio, *m'o ddicite mò?*" Maria jumps from Italian to Neapolitan, which leaps from her mouth with the force of a slap.

The shorter Neapolitan is, the more razor-sharp it gets. Don Ciccio swallows in silence. Maria enters back into the fold of Italian. "Don Ciccio, would you like to eat with us? A plate of spaghetti?" Don Ciccio stands, thanks her. He has to go back downstairs to his office. "Be careful. I spoke to you like a father, since there's no fathers around here anymore." Maria turns back to the stove. I accompany Don Ciccio to the door, shake his hand, and thank him for his interest. "Be careful, kid, be careful," he says, and fixes his hat as he descends the stairs.

IN THE kitchen Maria says that no one should come between us. I tell her about the broken plates. "Obviously he's got too many." Marì, he's gone crazy. "No, he's just jumping the gun. You're not supposed to break your old things until the end of the year. He's breaking them now. He's the landlord, isn't he? The owner of the whole building. What are a few plates to him?" She pours sauce over the drained pasta. We sit down and eat beside each other. Our legs touch. I know that she's right. No one should come between us.

IN THE workshop Rafaniello finishes the last pair of shoes. He can't sit still at his bench. He raises his head, looks around the room, his eyes alarmed, and becomes even more birdlike, left behind by the ones that migrated. He won't be coming down to the shop anymore. On the night of the thirty-first we'll meet up by the washbasins, we've agreed. He asks me how the boomerang is. It's always with me, Don Rafaniè, I keep it ready to fly. He jerks his neck toward the door. I turn around just as Master Errico comes in. " 'A ricciola guagliò, this morning I caught a sea bass in the waters off Santa Lucia. It was still dark. I was trawling a loose fishing line and she caught me, she caught me, tugging so hard she cut my hand," and he showed me the bloody red cut. "I gave her some slack so I wouldn't break the hook, which was tiny. I let her wear herself out, and when she was tired I brought her in a little at a time, and when she was right up alongside the boat I lifted her up with the harpoon. Three kilos! Three kilos, kid! The sun was just breaking over the sea and the bass was shinier than the dawn. I'll be eating fish for a week. I'll leave the sarago alone until the New Year. This morning I'm going to cook the head. It's this big," and he measures it with his hands. Between his two palms he leaves enough space for a soccer ball.

I COMPLIMENT him. You're a specialist, Master Errico, a fishing cabinet maker. He likes that I call him a cabinet maker, but he shrugs it off. "I'm just a carpenter who likes to fish. Nothing special about that. You want to hear something special? Papele the sailor, the one who walks around with the basket of fish that he catches fresh every morning, well, one beautiful day during the war he went out to sea and came back with chickens. That's right, he was fishing for chicken! He went up to his customers with a basket full of chickens. 'Papè, did you change jobs?' they asked. 'No, *signùri,* I go out to sea every day.' Truth is that the Americans had arrived days after our uprising and ordered a halt to all fishing because of the danger of German mines in the bay. Papele went out with his boat anyway. He went right up under the American ships and they threw chickens into the sea that they'd been keeping under ice. That's how Papele became a chicken fisherman."

MASTER ERRICO'S in a good mood. He's doesn't say hello to Rafaniello right away, but then he says he's going to send a slice of sea bass his way. "Look at how the wardrobe has dried. It's all set." We screw in the hardware, handles, keyholes, and hinges. With the milling machine he prepares the slot for the lock. I bring the piece close to the machine. My good eye is careful, I keep my bad eye half closed so it can rest. We'll deliver the wardrobe after New Year's. While we're working I ask him about Don Ciccio, whether he was a good man, too. "Good and brave. He was just a kid during the war and he helped the resistance fighters in secret. He ran errands for them during the bombardments, when no one was on the streets. I never saw him come down to the air-raid shelters." I also ask him whether he remembers Don Ciccio's sister. "What do you know about Don Ciccio's sister, kid?" Not much, Master Errico, I only know what he told me, that she ran errands. "Her errand was to go to the landlord, a married man who was free with his hands. She was a girl, a beautiful little girl." He lights his half cigar, meaning he has nothing more to say.

~ ~ ~

AT THE end of the day I close the shop. I accompany Rafaniello home. I take his arm. He walks with difficulty. Don Rafaniè, in a few months things have started happening fast, you and your hump, me and my job. My body's grown, my voice has gotten deeper. Where are the two of us running to? I ask, and with his little voice he answers, "Where I'm from we tell a joke about a rider who's having a hard time staying on a horse that's galloping through a field. A peasant asks him where he's going and he shouts back, 'Ask the horse.' " I smile, I don't get it, I laugh anyway. Rafaniello is so light you can pick him up. His bones must be hollow. There's air in his jacket. I see the curve of his folded wings and pass my hand over him to cover them better. In Naples people call the hump a *scartiello*. They think that stroking it brings you good luck. People are always putting their hands on Rafaniello's hump without asking permission. He lets them. "In my hometown they called me *gorbùn* and no one would even brush against me.

Here I like the familiarity that people have with my hump. I don't think I've brought anyone good luck, but all those strokes have helped me. They've awakened my wings."

DON RAFANIÈ, I could use a few strokes on my throat to get my voice back. My old voice is dead and my new one is stuck. He smiles and tells me that my voice will come all at once, and it'll be strong. He tells me a story. "When I was coming down into Italy after the war, I was walking along a country road when behind me I heard a terrifying scream, a harrowing cry, a begging so heart-rending that it made your ears bleed. I set my bags on the ground, turned around, and for the first time ever saw a donkey pulling a cart and a man beating it. The animal was straining its neck. With its harness tight and the bit in its mouth, it was howling in pain, so loud you could hear it for miles. If only I knew how to pray that way. In the Scriptures there are many passages about donkeys. It's a revered, hardworking animal. But its cry is useless, gigantic, something between it and God, it excludes mankind. It was May. My ears had had enough of the war, enough of horrible sounds. Inside my hump I felt a chill. All of a sudden my eyes were brimming with tears. Throughout the war my eyes had been dry. It took a country road in Italy and the cries of a donkey to awaken them. When your voice comes out it will have the force of a donkey." Thank you for the blessing, Don Rafaniè. The dark voice I've got now makes me sound like a conspirator. Did you know, Don Rafaniè, that the Naples soccer team has a donkey on its banner? It must be because whenever there's a goal the crowd at the stadium shouts as loud as a donkey. I heard the shout of the stadium once when I was walking by and tears came to my eyes, without my realizing it. That cry was overwhelming. It

was more important than scoring a goal, more powerful. In the meantime our conversation had brought us
to his room. I lit his candle and we said good night with
a nod of our heads.

I GO up to the washbasins to practice. There isn't much
of a moon, just a flicker of a fishtail over Vesuvius. It's
too low to use as a target. I aim for a higher star, close
my good eye, go through the motions of throwing,
counting out the number of attempts in my head till I
reach two hundred. The boomerang is curved. My
shoulders make a curve and my wrist makes one, too.
All together they're going to combine into one big push
forward. A combustion of muscle and nerve will un-
leash a long spinning hurl that will split heaven and
earth. The boomerang is hot, sharpened from all the
throws I've held back, waiting for my fingers to

open so it can rise through the darkness. My bad eye sees the sky close up. What will it take to fly? I think of Rafaniello and already see the sky lowering its drawbridge to let him and the boomerang pass. Every night it's a little lower and then all it will take is a jump from the terrace to reach it. The sky itself will beat your wings, Don Rafaniè, you won't have to make any effort, just keep them open. With my bad eye I get a good look at what's going to happen in the future.

EVEN IN the cold I sweat as my muscles whip through the air. A few swift caresses dry my face. The spirits like to lick the body's salts, enjoying the taste of freshly squeezed life, whipped into a froth. But when the body bleeds, they want no part of it. They rush to stop it, to press against the wound, drying cuts in a second. My bad eye takes aim at a star in the sky directly above the Castel dell'Ovo, a point to remember on the night of the thirty-first.

MARIA WANTS to go to the movies, to the Lux, where they're showing a picture with Totò. Totò is in the desert, shouting, "This tremendous African sun," and we laugh. Why do we laugh? Because we're at the movie theater sitting in the back, because we waited, standing, until two seats were free, because it's the first time that we've gone somewhere together, because the darkness tickles us, because sometimes people just laugh, so we laugh too at the voice of Totò that gets his mouth so out of joint when he speaks that he has to knock his chin back into place. Maria laughs the hardest. After everyone else has stopped she keeps on laughing, and her laughter makes them crack up all over again. Nothing very funny happens in the movie but everyone laughs at Maria's laughter, which she releases like a machine gun, in short broken bursts. A man sitting in front of us starts laughing so hard right after Maria that it sounds like he's choking. He sucks in his laugh with a wheeze, as if he were ready for the hospital. *"Chisto mo' more."* This one's gonna die, a woman behind us says, but nothing stops him, he's pissing himself, and when he comes up for a breath, Maria surprises him from behind with another peal of laughter, and he cracks up again with a pained whinnying, "He-he-he," and the theater bursts out with another volley that's got nothing to do with what's happening on the screen.

OUTSIDE THE theater everyone's happy, even though it's raining and no one thought to bring an umbrella. An old man laughs when he remembers the laughter. A woman says, *"Accussì adda essere 'o mbruoglio int'o len-zulo, c'adda fa' spassà!"* That's how the shenanigans be-tween the sheets should be, they should make us laugh! Neapolitans call the movies the shenanigans between the sheets because the real word is too strange, they have a hard time saying it, and they're afraid they're going to stutter, *"Cimetanocrafo."* *'O imbruoglio int'o len-zulo* is more to the point and better describes how a movie is a trick of light projected on a screen, a sheet. Maria places her arm in mine and we walk in the rain, refreshed by our laughter. At home on the bed in the closet it's crowded, uncomfortable. Maria says, "We're better off here, we're warm." She means we don't need to take advantage of the big bed. We make space for each other, one inside the other, and fall asleep cuddled up after a good dose of kisses. I've learned to relax my lips. I used to keep them as hard as a callus.

~ ~ ~

MARIA DOESN'T mind my smoky voice. She says she likes it, that she wants to hear it when we're kissing each other. Ask me something and I'll answer, I tell her. She laughs, saying, "Do you know my name?" I answer but she insists. "Repeat my name, repeat it," and I kiss her and say her name and it's love all over again and she likes it so much when I say her name that she thrashes and sobs with her whole body. Maria must be a magic name. She goes straight from kisses to sleep in the time it takes for my *piscitiello* to go back down. I no longer have to ask, *"Arò si' gghiuto?"* Where did you go? Now I know. I say her name a few more times, and she breathes in through her nose, swallows, and snores ever so softly.

~ ~ ~

I WAKE up. She's in the kitchen. She's boiled some water and she's pouring it over a coffee filter. At her house they use a moka machine that makes the coffee come out the top. I tell her that if the coffee goes up it's already tired when it arrives. Maria laughs. Very funny, she says. Truth is, I was only sharing an affectionate thought about coffee that I've only just gotten to know and that I like a lot, black with no sugar. I leave money on the table to buy what's missing from the kitchen. I put on the boomerang, my working jacket, and go down to the shop to open the gates. Mama, I think as I go downstairs, hurry home because I've got to ask you some stuff about women. It's cold. A northern chill in the stairwell makes me close my eyes, and I realize that the answer is no. Papa arrives at the workshop. Master Errico walks up to him. He's crying. I stand there with the broom in my hand. I squeeze it tight and keep my good eye closed so that I'll see everything out of focus and I won't see Papa's face. He's ashamed of crying in front of me. Master Errico takes the broom from my hands, pulls it away from me. We go out. He closes the workshop in mourning and goes to the hospital with us. Mama's not there. They've closed her in the coffin. I keep my arms close to my chest so that I'll get some warmth from the boomerang. The smell of *sfogliatelle* comes from a nearby bed. A man opens up a bag of pastries and offers us some. That's when the teardrops burst, now I know how to say it in Italian, because they come out and burst from your eyes with a shot from inside, a shot that forces them out.

MY FATHER'S stopped crying. His face is drained. He pays no attention to the people who come and speak to him and shake his hand or mine. I keep my good eye half closed and make myself look the way I'm supposed to for the procession of people from Montedidio. Then Maria arrives. She goes straight to Papa, takes him by the arm, and accompanies him outside. He goes with her quietly to get some fresh air and I stay behind to stand guard over the body of my mother, who didn't even want me to see her. Maria's parents came back home to get their suitcases. When they didn't find her, they left her some money and asked Don Ciccio to look after her. They have to take an emergency trip, they'll be back soon. "They're in trouble," says Maria, who heard about my mother from Don Ciccio. She did the shopping and came home to prepare something hot for us to eat. We leave the hospital. Papa's in the middle. He doesn't once look up from his feet. We guide him down the narrow sidewalks, where people are packed together as tight as olives in a jar. He's gotten thinner, and lets himself be moved about by us and by the wind that slaps our faces and makes them tougher.

~ ~ ~

MARIA MAKES a *maccheroni* frittata. I set the table. Papa sits down stiffly on the edge of a chair. His hands are on his knees. This way they can keep still. He's leaning over his legs a little. Teardrops break away from his nose and drop straight to the floor. Maria turns the frittata out onto his plate directly from the skillet, saying, "It's ready." Papa moves his chair in and quietly eats his whole portion. Maria sees the empty plate and fills it again without asking him. He finishes it. The more he chews the more the muscles in his face, his eyes, and his brow start to move again. Maria says that the shopkeepers raise their prices at Christmas and take advantage of people who want to make a good impression once a year. "We have to do the shopping in mid-August." The only thing Papa pays attention to is his plate. He cleans it with a piece of bread. Then he stands up and says he's got to go to the porters' cooperative to start working again. He tells me to buy a flask of wine, leaves me three hundred liras. Maria clears the table, washes up, puts things away. Maria does things quietly, proving that she knows how to run a kitchen and that even with a sad life you have to keep busy. At least that way there's no dirt, which would be one more offense. Instead everything's in order, even with tears in your eyes.

THE AFTERNOON is free. I tell Maria that we should go to Mergellina, where there's a pier that stretches into the sea. At its far end is a lighthouse and a reef, where you can be outdoors without the city around you. I want to go there because the houses, the streets, everything stops, and suddenly Naples is gone. The open sea and the crashing of the waves conceal it. All you have to do is walk down the pier. Maria puts on her coat. Her scarf is already hanging on the door. Her readiness soothes my bones. On the promenade I buy her a pork-fat-and-pepper *tarallo*. The wind carries away our warmth. We get it back by walking quickly. Not many people dare to take the walk. American soldiers in rubber shoes hurry by. The aircraft carrier in the bay is the only ship that doesn't move on the choppy sea spiked with whitecaps. Maria looks at the American soldiers and says, "They're a beautiful race but they're always running, running for nothing, for no reason. We Neapolitans have to be thrown out of our homes by an earthquake before we start running." Maria, why don't we run, too? "Noooo," she says, and with her arm she pulls me back into step with her.

AT THE Mergellina pier the riggings on the sailing ships are whistling. The dogs are scared. They hide under the fishermen's boats in dry dock. The two of us are the

only ones to go out on the pier that juts into the middle
of the dark sea. The boulders of the breakwater throw
water in the air, the waves crash, stop short, and split
apart by the bucketful. The boomerang underneath my
jacket trembles in the forceful air, pressing its electricity
against me. I'd like to throw it against the sea, the north
wind, the aircraft carrier, and everything that moves,
but not at my mother, no, she can no longer move.
Stand still, all of you, stop in your tracks for a minute:
if only I had a sliver of voice in my throat to make
myself heard, a voice that the wind could spread over
the city and make it stand still for a minute. Maria holds
my arm tight. I don't slip away from her, don't remove
the knot of my fist from the handle of the boomerang.
At the end of the pier the lighthouse is the farthest point
from the city, which seems to have come to a stop. I'm
pleased to see it quiet for a minute. A few lights flicker
from the island across the bay, from the towns on the
coast. Naples's shoulders are protected from the wind
and you can't hear a thing. I swallow big gulps of sea
air. Maria says, "Let's go back."

~ ~ ~

PAPA RETURNS home for supper. He sees the wine and before pouring himself some to drink he tries to explain, in Italian, "As long as she was alive I guarded her life, I snatched her away from death day and night." He drinks it down and says sharply, *"Mò nun pozzo fa' niente cchiù."* Now there's nothing more I can do. Maria nods her head. I'm just happy that he's searching for peace. He stayed with Mama till her last breath, and didn't want to go one step farther, not even to the cemetery. He pours himself another glass, asks if we're drinking, too. Maria says yes, I say no. She sips a couple of drops from the glass to taste it. Papa tells her, "That's not a sip, it's a breath. You're teasing the wine that way." Maria makes up for it by draining the glass with a flick of her wrist. We eat slowly, you can hear noises from the other homes. Papa drinks, passes his hand over his face, rubs his forehead. "Thanks for the supper." He gets up, says good night. In bed we lie close to each other but don't embrace. She says that her blood is running but it's not a cut, it's a change that women go through. She drank the wine to get her blood back. Before falling asleep, she says the precious words, "I care for you." As usual I don't know what to say in return.

MASTER ERRICO and Rafaniello said good-bye to each other when I wasn't there. It's the last day of the year. Tomorrow's a holiday, so today we have to work hard. We put all of the rough wood for the upcoming jobs through the planer. We make a lot of noise but today the neighborhood doesn't pay us any mind. No one sticks their head into the shop to ask Master Errico if he can keep it down, if he can do it later, because someone in the house that night didn't get any sleep, *"nun ha potuto azzecca' uocchio."* In an alley you try to run the machines at a time that doesn't disturb anyone. Today everyone's busy getting ready for the holiday so they don't mind the screeching of the blades that shave millimeters off the boards and splinter them into sawdust. Master Errico double-checks the squaring, corrects it, divides the finished boards by their grain. He grumbles about the lumberjack, who didn't cut the lumber during the right phase of the moon and now the wood is weak and bleeding resin. Master Errico tells me that Rafaniello is leaving, he got himself a ticket to sail to the Holy Land because he's a worshiper of Jerusalem. People don't get their shoes fixed in Montedidio anymore, he says, nowadays they buy them new or they're given to them by the mayor at election time, one before and one after the vote. I forget everything, think of work, and bury myself in sawdust. The boomerang is on my chest, beating against my heart. We don't even stop for lunch. We stop at four o'clock, when evening has already fallen. We wish each other a Happy New Year. Master Errico gives me double pay. "You earned it, kid, be well." Do you shoot a gun at midnight? I ask him. No, he says. He stands on the balcony, smokes a Tuscan cigar, and watches other people's fireworks. He likes the Roman candles. "Don Ciccio sets off the best Roman candles in Montedidio."

I SHAKE the sawdust off my clothes, beating myself like a rug. The boomerang bumps against my ribs and rustles like the wings beneath Rafaniello's jacket. I think of him. Tonight the flight of the boomerang will accompany him. At home my writing reaches the end of the scroll. A few more turns and nothing more will be left. I have to hold the scroll open, since the written part pulls it closed. I sharpen my pencil and wait for Maria, who's gone out. She comes back out of breath. She went up to her place to clean up and to get a change of clothes. The landlord was waiting for her at the door and threw himself on her right in the middle of the staircase. She didn't shout. She kicked him in the shins and got away. "If you had been there you would have thrown him down the stairs," she says. She's agitated, frightened. He was holding her tight with his hands and his breath stank. He's out of his mind, but she defended herself. My thoughts become dark, my nerves frayed, wound tight from the boomerang. They want to shove and slap everyone in sight. *Maria, nun succere n'ata vota.* It won't happen again. These grim words come out in my Neapolitan voice. I show my ugly side. It's the first time, so I don't know what kind of a face I've just made, because Maria takes it in her hands and says, "Don't act like that. Forget about it. It's over already. It was nothing, I shouldn't even have told you." She looks for my eyes and I don't know where I put them because she tells me, "Look at me, look me in the face," and moves my face until I let go of the dark thoughts, look at her, take her wrists, and give myself two slaps in the face with them, clenching my teeth. She gets scared and hugs me and now yes, now it's all over.

IT WON'T happen again, I tell her, but not in Neapolitan. I tell her quietly so she'll calm down. Today I've learned something about myself, something sad in the middle of my good luck at being with Maria. Not everything is good about my body growing. Something evil grows up alongside it. Alongside myself, alongside the strength of my arms to free the boomerang, grows a bitter force capable of violence. A sulfur pond has started boiling inside my head, making my thinking evil. Is this what men suddenly become? Someone makes a bad move, you blow your stack, and out comes the evil blood. Papa comes home. Maria asks him if tonight he'd like pizza, we'll go get some at Dirty Gigino's, who makes the best pizza in the neighborhood. Right away he says yes, a pizza margherita. Same thing for us. So we lay the tablecloth on the marble table in the kitchen. When we come back we'll eat it while it's still hot. He's tired. Today he worked in the bottom of the hold without a break, something the older workers don't do. He sits down with the newspaper on his knee. The lightbulb is twenty watts. He tries to read, straining his eyes.

THEN WE go out, saying see you later. He doesn't answer. He reads, moving his lips to follow the words. Maria and I know how to read better than him. It's not fair. We, the late-comers, who had the luxury to study, we know more than a strong adult man who made sure his whole life that we didn't want for the basics and who was always respectful to his wife. I close the door behind us, letting Maria out first. I feel honored by my father, who has to move his lips to read. Marì, we have to buy the best pizza in Naples. "We wouldn't go out for less. At the very least the best in Naples, then we'll see if it isn't the best in the world." Maria, I tell her, I care for you. "Those are my words. You have to use your own," she answers, leaving me looking stupid once again.

DIRTY GIGINO is making pizza for all of Naples. There's a crowd in front of his store. It's cold and he's standing there in his undershirt slapping the dough around and spinning it absentmindedly. He calls out to the crowd, *"Song 'e ppizze 'e sott 'o Vesuvio, nc'è scurruta 'a lava 'e ll'uoglio."* He's saying that there's as much oil on his pizza as there is lava running down the slopes of Vesuvius. This way people don't mind waiting as much, because they work up an appetite from Don Gigino's exaggerated words. They call him dirty—*'o fetente*—because he has a beard and sometimes you find dark hairs in your pizza. He wears a beard because his face is scarred. I stand off to the side on the sidewalk. Maria goes up to the counter and lets her voice be heard good and loud: "Don Gigì, three of your pizza margheritas 'cause we want to cheer ourselves up," she shouts out in the midst of the crowd, letting loose her fresh, flirtatious side. *"Nenne', i' m'arricreo quanno te veco."* I cheer up whenever I see you, Don Gigino responds from the counter, with his dark beard, eyes, and hair, dusted in flour like an anchovy. He rushes us ahead of the others, handing us three pizzas, one on top of the other, with wax paper in between. He shouts for everybody to hear, *"Facite passa' annanze 'a cchiù bella guagliona 'e Montedidio!"* Make way for the most beautiful girl in Montedidio! and Maria makes her way through the crowd and takes the pizzas from the hands of Don Gigino, who even tells her she can pay for them another time.

"Cheste m'e ppave ll'anno che vene." Maria, walking tall and brash from the honor, comes to me, puts her arm in mine, and we walk up to Montedidio with people's eyes on our backs. It's so important to be two, a man and a woman, in this city. He who's alone is less than one.

ON THE street firecrackers are going off and people are rushing home to get ready for the party. The pizzas are smoking in Maria's hands. Her footsteps sound like wood. I realize she's wearing high-heeled shoes. It's just that I saw Maria was taller and didn't look at her shoes. At first I thought that she grew quickly from one day to the next. Now I see the heels, but I still know anyway that she's taller, even without them. We race forward. Quickly we find ourselves high atop Montedidio, where we can look at the stars face-to-face. Don Gigino sees us and lets us pass in front of all his customers, because he sees us running, growing and running. Maria is taller. Her figure has shot up from a girl's to a woman's, everyone who sees her notices. I don't say a thing. Whatever she does is fine with me.

AT HOME Papa's asleep with the newspaper on his legs. I take it away, he wakes up, looks around himself in a daze, passes a hand over his face, and says, "I thought I was at your mother's bedside." Maria doesn't give him time to think about it. "Supper's on the table," she calls, clattering the plates. I take my jacket off, set the boomerang on the table. "You've still got it? So you liked it. I'd forgotten," and while he cuts himself a slice of the juiciest pizza in Naples and maybe in the world, he asks me whether it flies. "Like pizza in the hands of Don Gigino," Maria answers, but he's already chewing and has forgotten. I tell him how Don Gigino served us before all the other people who were waiting. "He used to do the same for us. Don Gigino likes seeing married couples," he remembers, without thinking. He drinks a glass of wine, pours one for Maria, says that he's not going to stay up until midnight. He cracks a walnut, crushing it in his hand, chews it with relish. Mama liked almonds, there aren't any, I didn't buy them. At the table you need a little mourning.

HE TOOK a colleague's shift. Tomorrow he's going in for another guy, who's staying home on New Year's Day. He wants to work and wear himself out. He says he's really happy to come home to a hot meal. He gets up, says good night, and then at the kitchen door turns around and says, "Thanks for the pizza." Maria smiles at him and my eyesight gets blurry. I swallow, turn around, pick up the boomerang, and squeeze it to calm down. Everything is moving too fast, I can't manage to keep up, everything changes from one hour to the next. He said, "thank you" for so little, even though the life he knew is over, and outside they're setting off fireworks, making one year new and throwing out the old one, and with all his heart he's still inside the years that have passed, that are thrown out, they're all mixed together. I start clearing the table. Maria washes the dishes and outside the merrymaking grows. For one night the city imitates Vesuvius expelling fire and flame. We turn the light out, look out at the other windows, look down on the street.

ON MY chest the boomerang beats against the pulsing of my blood. Maria places her ear between my shoulder and neck and repeats softly, "Boom, boom, your heart's even racing when you're still. Inside your chest a rascal is throwing stones against a wall." I close my good eye. The balconies and lighted windows across the way recede even more, becoming street lamps in the dark. Boom, boom, to live you have to have a pulse, to fly, to break away from the earth, to ascend the sky on air, a strong pulse. "Boom, boom, boom," Maria continues. Her voice draws blood to my stomach, saliva to my mouth. Maria, I tell her, at midnight I'm going up to the washbasins. I'm going to throw the boomerang. "I'm coming with you." Rafaniello will fly and all the spirits will come to see him off. Our spirits are curious. They'll want to brush against a flying shoemaker. Spirits don't know how to fly. They can only create a little breeze. Firecrackers are going off on the street. Maria doesn't hear what my dark voice is saying. She's thinking of her blood. "The wine was good for me. It's the first time I've had it, it's good. I liked the way he poured it. He held the heavy flask steady and made it come out very slowly."

~ ~ ~

MARIA'S BEAUTIFUL with the blood she's losing, the wine that's replacing it, her black hair tickling my neck and her mouth that goes boom, boom, opening and closing with her kisses. To imitate the sound of my heart she blows kisses to the dark. We stay at the window; in the meantime the frenzy of fireworks rises, people in Montedidio are setting off firecrackers everywhere. The blasts even come from far away, from the marina. Rafaniello is in his storeroom, warming his wings. I tell Maria it's time to go up. We pull away from the window, the boomerang shifts from my rib to my heart. Let's go up, Marì. She slips under my arm, carelessly, lost in thought. The stairs echo with the ruckus, a gust of little drafts circles, celebrates, and tickles us, blowing their chilly New Year's greetings into our ears. They're fond of us, and I of them. Maybe even Mama made it in time to come, although spirits stay close to their bodies at first, keeping them company. Only later do they separate.

The landlord's door is open. Inside it's dark. Maria holds me tighter.

ABOVE THE terrace colored lights spread across the sky. They're shooting off rockets from rooftops and balconies, and it's not even midnight. I try to warm up my arms for the throw, they're ready, don't need a warmup, the boomerang's force belongs to me. I want to put enough into it to break my arm off. Which one? Right or left? Left, the side of my good eye, which I'll keep closed. I gaze up at the curtain of stars, looking for the one that I saw above the volcano. I spot it, it trembles more than the others. I point it out to Maria with the tip of the boomerang. It's in the east. I'm going to throw in that direction. Maria goes to the bulwark, leans on it with her elbows to see far away, she hears and doesn't hear. It must be the wine, the exhaustion, the blood. Rafaniello arrives, his wings are under a blanket, they don't fit into his jacket anymore. Don Rafaniè, how are you? He doesn't answer. He hugs me with the warmth of his feathers and tells me softly, *"Blib ghezìnt, be good,"* then slips his shoes off. Don Rafaniè, do you see that star, you and the boomerang will pass right under it, it'll blaze the path for you between the fireworks. Maria stands still, looking out, she doesn't turn around. All at once it is midnight, Naples is ablaze, shooting, breaking, throwing stuff into the street, you can't hear a single voice, everything is a burst of energy that shoots into the air, above the earth, against the walls. I squeeze the wooden handle in my hand.

IT BURNS in my hand. It does it deliberately. Otherwise at the last second I won't throw it. It scalds my fingers to make me throw it. I breathe on it. This only makes it worse. I tense up, my mouth snaps at the air, I take a deep breath, cock the boomerang back behind my shoulders, close my good eye, peer at the sky sparkling with light like an August sea shimmering with anchovies, the burning in my fingers forces the air out of my lungs, and with a crunching of bone the boomerang breaks away, its tail on fire, a thrust like never before, the wood burns, floats, flies, whips through the air, there's nothing in my hands. Behind me bedsheets are flapping in the wind, but there are no sheets. I turn around, it's Rafaniello, his wings spread wide, his naked feet rising above the ground, they fall back down, once, twice, the wind rises, beaten by his wings, the spirits do their part to get up under him and push, and on the third jump Rafaniello rises and follows the blazing trail of the boomerang and the din of firecrackers, whistles, sending breezes spinning across my face, a celebration, and I raise my arms for one final push farewell.

~ ~ ~

I TOUCH my hand. It's stopped burning. It's new again. On the ground are Rafaniello's blanket, two feathers, and a pair of shoes. In the air are the fireworks, the rockets, echoing off the walls. Montedidio thunders, I open my good eye, Maria screams at a shadow, I run to the bulwark, grab the shadow by its shoulders, my arms burning with energy. I tear the shadow away from Maria and throw it away, throw it away so hard that it flies, flies from the terrace of Montedidio, flies through the deluge of old vases and plates thrown from the balconies, everything is flying from Montedidio, but not the two of us, the two of us hugging each other under Rafaniello's blanket, Maria shaking, me coughing up a hot clot of air from my throat. It's a voice, my voice, a donkey's braying that rips from my lungs. I shout, and there isn't enough room for my shout on my whole scroll of paper or even in the sky above Montedidio.

ABOUT THE AUTHOR

Erri De Luca was born in Naples in 1950. He is a columnist for *Il Manifesto* and a novelist whose work has been translated into seven languages. He lives outside of Rome.

ABOUT THE TRANSLATOR

Michael Moore is a New York–based writer, translator, and teacher. His previous translations include *The Silence of the Body* by Guido Ceronetti.